CONSUMED BY LOVE

WRITTEN IN THE STARS BOOK 10

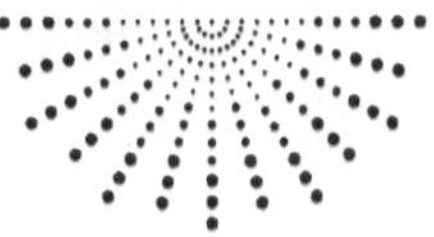

C.M. ALBERT

CONSUMED BY LOVE (Written in the Stars Book 10)
Genre: Contemporary Romance

Cover by Marisa Wesley of Cover Me Darling, LLC
Cover Photographer, Christopher John of CJC Photography
Cover Models, B.T. Urruela and Rachael Baltes
Editing by Crystal Shelley of Dot and Dash, LLC
Formatting by Stephanie Anderson of Alt 19 Creative

FOREWORD

WRITTEN IN THE STARS

Dear readers,

Do you believe in destiny? Or do you believe you drive your own fate when it comes to matters of the heart?

The idea for the Written in the Stars series came about one afternoon as I was thinking about how intertwined we are with the universe and the cosmos—we're made of stardust, after all. It got me thinking about astrology and whether something as celestial as our zodiac signs influence how we behave in love. Some may call it pseudoscience, while others use their horoscopes daily to make major life, love, and career decisions.

That's how this series was born!

Twelve months. Twelve wickedly talented romance authors. All coming together to answer the age-old question—Does your horoscope decide your fate in love?

You'll have to decide for yourself as you binge-read your way through twelve deliciously sexy and deeply romantic stand-alone novellas—one for each zodiac sign. I can't wait to start this journey with you. Personally? I think it was written in the stars!

XO,
C.M. Albert

P.S. Please join us in our fun and interactive Written in the Stars readers' group at https://www.facebook.com/groups/writteninthestarsbooks where we discuss all things horoscope and love related!

DEDICATION

This book is for my husband, Derek.

You are my best friend, my reward for being such a good girl, and my inspiration for being not such a good girl. You are every answer I have ever asked for from God, and it's clear to me that our love story was written in the stars many moons ago. I am so grateful to keep meeting you in each new lifetime, and I keep loving you more and more every time. We have the greatest love story never told. The one no one would believe, anyway. Ours.

CONSUMED BY LOVE PLAYLIST

2U (feat. Justin Bieber) – David Guetta
Always Tomorrow – Shane Filan
Amazed – Shane Filan
As Long as You Love Me – Ali Brustofski
Baby Blue Eyes – Olly Murs
Because of Me – Billy Gilman
Butterflies – Alex G
Completely – Shane Filan
Dreams – Bazzi
Eternal Flame – Shane Filan
Explosion – Nicky Byrne
Fetish – Alex Goot & Jada Facer
Head & Heart (feat. MNEK) [Acoustic] – Joel Corry
I Love You – Alex & Sierra
I Try – Ben Taylor
I Won't Let You Down – Alex Clare
I'm Yours – Alessia Cara
LoveStoned – Boyce Avenue
Marvin Gaye (feat. Meghan Trainor) – Charlie Puth
Perfect – Britton Buchanan
The Bright Side – Erick Baker
You Have My Heart – Anthem Lights

"Consumed by the light of her love,
I forgot to thank darkness
for how it answered my wish of
procuring her,
by sacrificing one of its own
shimmering stars!"

—Pranav Hegde

"You are my sun, my moon, and all my stars."

—E.E. Cummings

"Seduce my mind and you can have my body.
Find my soul, I'm yours forever."

—Anonymous

PROLOGUE

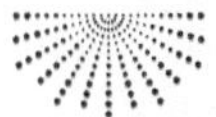

SCORPIO

Your Daily Horoscope for

Friday, October 29

TODAY IS GOING to be a great day, Scorpio woman! You've been in a slump lately, but once again, you will rise from the ashes! Your career will take a turn for the better, and your love life is about to get so hot you'll need to be careful not to get burned!

A dark stranger will cross your path today—and he just might wield the arrow that pierces your protected heart and captures it for good! But with romance on the horizon, don't overlook the gifts staring you right in the face. There may be an even better prospect coming soon, a second chance that will tip your good fortune in love—maybe forever.

Either way, your forecast is looking hot, Scorpio! It's time for this passionate, fiery sign to get a taste of its own medicine and finally be consumed—by love, that is.

Are you ready for it?

It was written in the stars.

CHAPTER ONE

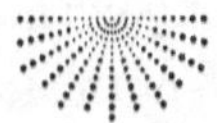

I CHEWED ON THE wood casing of my red pencil, something I often did when I was stuck during a particularly challenging edit. It wasn't that the author's manuscript was *bad* just because it was now giving me indigestion. But if I had to cross out the word "throbbing" one more time and write "WC" next to it to let the author know she needed to choose another word, I would absolutely lose my shit.

I flung my pencil across my desk and stood, stretching the aches from my lower back. I was wracking my brain for an alternative word when my best friend, Lindy, popped her perky blond head into my office from the doorway.

"Ooh! I'm glad you're here!" I said, frantically searching for another red pencil. I always had one somewhere. I reached for my hair and laughed as I pulled out the one that I'd tucked behind my ear earlier. I was such a cliché.

"What's another word for 'throbbing'?"

Lindy snorted. "Pulsing? Aching? Swollen?" She wiggled her eyebrows at me. "You have all the fun down here in romance," she complained. "Ooh! I got it! What about engorged?"

Our eyes met, and we both burst out laughing. "Engorged, huh? Since when does 'engorged' sound sexy to you?"

"Well, if—"

"Okay, okay. I get it. But I'm not suggesting that word," I said, eyeing her. "You got your hair cut, didn't you?"

Her almost shoulder-length blond bob fell in soft waves, and she had super short new bangs that only Lindy could rock. It was very forties-esque.

Lindy nodded and ran her plum-colored nails through her hair. "Do you like it?" she asked, fidgeting with her bangs. "I'm still getting used to the fringe again."

"Has Walter seen it yet?" I asked. Walter was her current love interest, who happened to be much, much older than she was—and much wealthier too.

Lindy grinned, the apples of her cheeks flaming a bright red. "He actually suggested it."

"Well, I think you look smoking hot, and obviously he does too," I said, arching a brow. "Very coquettish."

Lindy snorted again. "Only you could pull out 'coquettish' in a normal conversation," she teased. "Come on, though, or we're going to be late. Carlisa is making her big announcement today." She squealed and tugged my arm to get me moving.

I grabbed my laptop and closed the door behind us as we headed to our weekly wrap-up meeting. They were usually dull, with each division's senior editor covering their status on their current authors' edits and discussing any new queries from book agents that we were on the fence about. Sometimes we had to pass a lead on to a different division because it was really inspirational fiction instead of contemporary romance, that kind of thing. Our meetings usually ended with the entire senior staff heading downstairs to the upscale cigar bar on the first floor of our office building to share a drink and celebrate the weekend.

But today was different. Today was the day I'd been waiting for, for a long time. Hopefully, I'd be celebrating a lot more than just the weekend.

As Lindy and I took our seats around the conference room table and waited for everyone to trickle in, she tapped on her phone and showed it to me. "What do you think of this?" she whispered.

I looked down at the strapped harness made of red leather that I could only assume was some sort of bodysuit. There wasn't enough material to actually cover anything, so it had to feel like solving a puzzle when climbing into it.

"It's hot," I admitted. "What's it for?"

"I'm wearing it under my costume tomorrow night for the Heart Gala," she said. "Think Walter will like it?"

"I think Walter will absolutely salivate over it, Lindy. But aren't you worried about giving the poor man a heart attack?"

She giggled and swatted my arm. "He's not *that* old."

It was my turn to snort back at her. "Yeah, but he's not that *young* either," I reminded her, nodding as the other editors took their places around the table.

There was a lot of talent at the table, but none nearly as capable as I was to fill Carlisa's shoes when she went on maternity leave. It was my opportunity to prove I could step into her role permanently when she returned and took over as CIO—*if* she returned. There was already a pool going on about that one.

"Seriously, Lindy," I said, glancing down at the picture one last time, "I hope you're covering that thing at the gala.

Otherwise you'll end up on the front page of the *Observer* and looking for a new job by lunch time come Monday."

"I'll have something over most of it," she insisted as she scrolled through her phone again. "Just the straps are going to show. Oh, I almost forgot! Here's your daily horoscope."

Lindy handed me her phone, and I took it greedily. We both obsessed over our horoscopes and read them together most days.

"Do you still have time to get a drink at Havana's after work?" I asked. We tried hard not to break our weekly Friday night ritual, even if it was just one drink.

"I think so. Guess it depends on how long Cruella blows hot air up there today," she said, not at all trying to be quiet. Our hunky non-fiction editor, Dan, chuckled. He lifted his coffee to his lips as our eyes met. I grinned back before reading my horoscope.

"Well, that sounds ominous," I said, glancing down at the zodiac prediction screenshotted on Lindy's phone.

"What's so ominous about it?" she whispered back. "I think it's exciting, don't you? You've literally been wanting Carlisa's job for, what, the past seven years? And today of all days you get a horoscope like *that?*"

It sure would be nice if my job took a turn for the better today. I reread my horoscope one last time, doing a double take at the ending.

Are you ready for it? It was written in the stars.

Shivers ran over my entire body as I closed my eyes, dreaming of hearing those magic words: "Brynn will be taking over my job while I'm on maternity leave." My scalp tingled as goose bumps raced up my arms. Maybe that's why I missed the clipped words actually coming from Carlisa's mouth. I watched as her lips moved in slow motion, everyone turning to stare at me before she moved on to the weekly division briefings.

What just happened?

The conference room was abnormally quiet as we each gave our updates. After the meeting was over, Lindy grabbed my hand and hauled me down the hallway to my office, closing my door behind us. I sat on the edge of my desk, feeling numb.

"I didn't get it, did I?" I whispered.

"It's okay, Brynn. There will be another chance. You know this was just a temporary solution to judge fit until she moves over to the CIO role."

"Yeah, but I can't prove I'm fit if I don't have the job."

Lindy bit the corner of her lip, neither agreeing nor disagreeing.

"Did they say who got it? I completely spaced out," I groaned. "Please tell me it wasn't Shay." That was my archnemesis from the sweet romance division. How the Wicked Witch of the West could curate sweet and clean romance novels was beyond me.

"No. She just said it was an outsider, and we'll find out Monday who it is."

"Great," I muttered, locking up the half-finished manuscript that I'd left on my desk, mid-edit, before the staff meeting. It was my birthday weekend, so there was no way I was bringing work home. Besides, how much would that suck to have to *read* about things throbbing, while not actually getting to experience it firsthand on my birthday?

"I'm a mess, Lindy. I need something tall, dark, and—"

"Throbbing?" she teased, winking at me.

"Exactly. That's exactly what I need. To get laid for my birthday," I joked. I swung my laptop bag over my shoulder and turned off my lights. "Shots?"

We linked arms and headed down to Havana's. That was what I loved about Lindy. The damn girl was always there for me no matter what. I needed to get my head out of the clouds. The stupid horoscope was wrong. My career hadn't taken a turn for the better. Piercing arrows? Second chances?

More like bullshit.

CHAPTER TWO

THE LONG WALK to the elevator banks was especially awkward. A few people had trouble meeting my eyes, and you could've heard a pin drop on the main floor. Great! Everyone was talking about me. It was no secret that I'd been working toward Carlisa's role—everyone had to have an "up or out" strategy at Sterling and Masters. Her role was my "up," and the thought of being "out" made me nauseated.

Hushed whispers about an "outsider" followed us, along with noise about why the role wasn't being filled from within. Yeah, I needed that answer, too, but it would have to wait till Monday. There was no way I was confronting Carlisa right now. It took all my willpower to hold back the fiery Scorpio in me as I put work behind me for the night. I knew my bite could sting when I was provoked too hard. It was bad enough I didn't get the promotion; I certainly didn't need to lose my job on top of that.

As we entered the elevators, I met the cold, calculating eyes of my nemesis. Because, of course, Shay had to be there. A smug grin lifted the corners of her lips when she saw us.

My insides tightened, but I vowed to play nice—for as long as I could.

"You headed down for drinks?" I asked and pressed the L button. Lindy squeezed my arm in solidarity, or warning. I wasn't sure.

"You're actually going tonight?" she asked, balking. Her admin, who was standing next to her clutching a stack of books, snickered. I wanted to punch him in his scrawny little rat face.

"Why wouldn't I? We go every Friday, and it's my birthday weekend." I exhaled as I stepped off the elevator, wanting to get as much distance as I could from Shay. But the red-headed witch followed us into the bar and stood right next to me and Lindy as I waited to order.

"Why don't we do tequila shots?" she said, unusually friendly for once. I eyed her skeptically. I could read people in a way that made others nervous, but Shay didn't know that. And right now, my Bullshit Barometer was zinging off the charts.

"Are you going to the Heart Gala?" Lindy asked her.

Please say no. Please say no.

She eyed me, narrowing her gaze.

Just then, the bartender slid our shots across the sleek black bar top. Shay passed one to me and one to Lindy before lifting her own glass in the air. "Here's to Carlisa's new replacement. May it be a man. A really hot man. And may Carlisa decide to stay home and push out more babies!"

Lindy cleared her throat and side-eyed me, shaking her head. I didn't raise my glass in return. I just threw back the tequila and ordered another. Holy shit, that burned!

Ordering another was probably not the smartest idea, especially since I needed to pick up my costume tonight for the gala. But I was in a dangerous mood after getting rejected.

"To new beginnings and exciting second chances," Lindy said and winked at me.

I grinned back. She was always so much more optimistic than I was, but the damn pixie rubbed off on me. She was the exact yin to my yang that I needed in my life. "To surprises going over well at the gala," I answered in turn, thinking of her sexy costume addition.

Shay glowered at us, as if offended that we were sharing inside jokes she wasn't privy to. It seemed as if we constantly rubbed Shay the wrong way. I wish I could say that bothered me, but I couldn't trust her as far as I could throw her, so she certainly didn't inspire me to bring her into our fold. I couldn't figure out what she was even doing hanging out with us. She hated us, and the feeling was mutual.

Dan came through the doors to the cigar bar, and his eyes zeroed in on Lindy. She groaned, and I elbowed her. That's when I noticed a sly look fill Shay's ice-blue eyes as she drank Dan in from head to toe.

Bingo.

"Hello, ladies!" Dan said, wrapping an arm over Lindy's shoulder, which elicited yet another scowl from Shay. "What's on tap tonight?"

"Tequila shots," I said and raised the second one I ordered. "I've decided to live dangerously since it's my birthday weekend!" I was already feeling the happy effects of my first shot. The second one didn't burn any less going down.

"And to drown out her sorrows," Shay added.

"What is actually your problem?" I asked, narrowing my eyes at her. "If you have something to say, please be an adult and just say it."

I watched as the cold calculation spun behind her eyes and fake Southern sweetness took its place.

"I don't know what you mean, Brynn," she said.

Shay placed her hand on Dan's free arm and trailed her fingers over his bare skin. Like most men in the bar, his work sleeves had already been pushed up to his elbows for the evening, and his tie dangled loosely around his neck.

"Will you be at the Heart Gala tomorrow night?" she cooed, her eyes unabashedly trying their best to lure Dan in. He was either oblivious to her attention or completely aware and too smart for the conniving witch.

Like a seasoned pro, he playfully spun Lindy out of his arms and then back in again, eliciting a laugh as she swatted him. "Only if Lindy promises me a dance."

"You're skating on thin ice, mister," she teased. Dan had had a crush on Lindy for as long as I could remember. The only problem? He was about thirty years and a couple million shy of Lindy's typical love interest.

"A man can always dream," he said, lifting her hand and kissing it, squarely in front of Shay.

Oh yeah. He was too smart for the likes of her.

"You know I'm dating Walter," Lindy said quietly.

He laughed and pulled her into a close embrace. I chuckled when I saw Shay's face burn bright red, her jaw clenching. "Walter won't be around forever," he said affectionately. "Doesn't he already have his AARP membership?"

She socked him in the arm. "That was rude!" she said, but she was laughing. She knew what others thought about her, and she didn't give two flying fucks either way. Lindy was happy with Walter. He met her needs in a way Dan simply couldn't. I kind of felt bad for the poor guy. He never stood a chance with her.

"Did you say whether you were going to the Heart Gala or not?" I asked Shay, who was fuming at this point. I watched as she tossed back another shot. Drunk Shay was a bad combo—we'd all witnessed her self-destruction at last year's Christmas party.

"Yeah, I think I'll go," she said, eyeing Dan as he joined a group of guys from the office who'd just walked in. Her eyes trailed his ass as the guys made their way to the smoking lounge in the cigar bar. Shay probably only wanted Dan because he *didn't* want her. As soon as she got her hooks in her most recent conquest—and proved she could—she'd drop him faster than last week's garbage. Casualties be damned.

I should know. I was once one of her casualties, thanks to my ex Nick.

I took a deep breath, finding myself needing space. And fresh air. I wanted out. Out of the bar. Out of Shay's presence. Away from *work.*

I turned to tell Lindy that I was ready to go when I slammed into something tall, dark, and made of steel. A firm hand gripped my wrist to prevent me from falling and making an ass of myself. When I looked up to see who my savior was, I found the smokiest midnight-blue eyes staring back at me. My heart pounded as they drank me in.

The man's dark brown hair was cut close, and even though he was in a monochrome navy suit as dark as his eyes, I could see the definition in his arm as he held me upright. My hands rested on a chest so hard it had no business being locked away behind the crisp white dress shirt he was wearing. I couldn't help but notice the ten pence lion cufflinks made of solid gold that held his French cuffs together. The man oozed sexuality and power, and a tiny part of me whimpered somewhere deep inside.

"I'm used to women falling fast for me," he growled in my ear, "but this is a record even for me."

I couldn't form a pithy response or look away to save my life, and I saw in the depths of his captivating orbs that he knew it. A cocky grin spread over his full red lips as he helped me stand upright on my own. The dark-haired god before me held up a finger to the entourage of men in suits waiting for him by the bar's exit.

"You steady enough on your feet to get home? Or do you need to crash at my place?" he said, his eyes raking over the small amount of cleavage that showed in my short black button-down dress. I slid my hands into the dress's pockets so I wouldn't be tempted to find out what else was made of steel on him. And I'd had just enough tequila to consider it.

"As tempting as your offer is, it's my birthday tomorrow. And waking up in a stranger's bed isn't exactly my idea of a good time." I made eye contact with Lindy, who had stepped away from the bar and was busy texting—presumably to Walter. He kept her on a short leash. Figuratively, and literally sometimes.

"That's because you've never woken up in *my* bed," he said, his navy eyes smoldering even darker.

I didn't know whether to laugh or grab his hand and run. A man with that kind of confidence probably *would* be my idea of a good time. Who was I fooling? Thank god, Lindy chose that moment to push her way into our little foray and grab my hand.

"Hey, handsome," she said, winking at the mystery man. "Hate to steal this hottie, but it's her birthday tomorrow, and we have things to do."

He chuckled. "So I've heard. Give me two minutes, and she's all yours."

Lindy raised her eyebrows at me, and I could tell that she was squealing inside. But she played it cool. "Two minutes, Casanova."

As she made her way to the front of the bar to wait for me, I couldn't help but notice Shay's icy gaze walking her out with glee. She spun on her heels and stalked toward the cigar bar, no doubt on the hunt for poor Dan.

I turned my attention back to the most beautiful man I'd ever laid eyes on. Whoever created the expression "butterflies in your tummy" had clearly never met my Casanova here. Butterflies were nowhere to be found in the burning ache that seared its way down my torso and between my thighs. He was standing too close. Smelled too much like expensive cologne and sex. He was a man used to getting anything he wanted.

"What did you need two minutes f—"

The shock of his lips on mine made me lose any coherence I had left. I grabbed the collar of his dress shirt to prevent myself from falling back again. The strong hand he'd used to grip my wrist a moment ago now cupped the back of my head, tangled up under my long dark brown hair. I knew I should push him away—I didn't even know his name. But it was my birthday weekend, and his mouth tasted exquisite. His lips were surprisingly soft as they crushed against mine, but his tongue was aggressive as he pressed between my lips, claiming my mouth with his. I may've whimpered. I may've come. All I know is that at some point, I dropped my hands to my sides and just let him devour me with his hot, demanding mouth.

Fuck.

When he pulled back, he ran a finger over my lower lip.

"Happy birthday, angel," he said, pressing something cold into my hand before turning and making his way back to his entourage. When he passed Lindy—who was standing there gaping at the way I'd just let a stranger manhandle me—he said something quietly into her ear before leaving the bar and never looking back.

It took me a few minutes to calm my breathing enough to snap the hell out of it and figure out what in the world just happened. Well, my horoscope had been right—I'd met a tall, dark stranger. The only problem was that I never got his name before I had the sexiest, most tantalizing kiss I'd had in a long, long time. It was a far cry from piercing my heart, but I'd take it as a win.

When I finally made my way across the bar to Lindy, she grabbed my hand so we could walk to the long line of cabs waiting outside. That's when I remembered Casanova had pressed something into my palm before leaving. I glanced down and laughed. It wasn't exactly a glass slipper or the start of a fairy tale romance.

Instead, it was a room key.

CHAPTER THREE

I SAT IN THE hot tub that consumed most of my back patio's square footage. The hot water and large glass of wine soothed my bruised ego from earlier today. After my surprise kiss, I'd headed straight home. I'd have to pick up my rental costume tomorrow.

The noisy bubbles danced around me, and I ran my teeth over my lower lip—the same one Casanova had sucked on between his own warm lips before ending our kiss. My skin tingled from the memory, and my nipples instantly hardened in the cool evening air. At least, I was blaming it on the temperature and not the magnetic pull I'd felt with my mystery man.

I still wasn't sure if I should've punched him for kissing me without asking, or march my way over to the Lion's Den hotel and let him prove me wrong about whether or not it would be a good time to wake up in his arms on my birthday. Right now, I was kind of kicking myself as I flipped his key card over and over in my hands, lost in the memory of his hot tongue pressing past my lips to seek out mine.

Holy hell.

Enough was enough. I checked the time, my head starting to ache from the tequila and large goblet of wine. The only thing worse than waking up in a stranger's bed on my birthday would be to wake up with a hangover from hell, unable to attend the annual Heart Gala with my friends.

I set the glass down on the edge of the hot tub, along with the room key. The gold lion's head mocked me from the front of the card, reminding me of the cufflinks he'd worn and the feel of his strong hands as they gripped my wrist. In one simple move, he'd stirred feelings of both protection and dominance, and I wasn't sure which one thrilled me more.

I closed my eyes, letting my hand slide over my breasts and down my flat stomach. Even though I had neighbors on either side of me, the lights were off on my patio, and I couldn't wait until I got inside. I dipped my hand beneath the water and started rubbing myself. The more I remembered his kiss, the harder I pressed my thighs together. I wasn't a one-night stand type of girl, but I certainly wasn't shy either. In fact, I took pride in my horoscope being one of the most passionate and sexual of all the zodiac signs.

As I rubbed my clit beneath the water, knowing just where and how hard to press down to push myself over the edge, I grinned. He might've caught me off guard, but if I'd taken him up on his offer, I'd have given him a run for his money. I knew it deep in my soul.

The sex would've been phenomenal.

I let my writer's imagination take over, helping me come quicker than I ever had before. That night, despite my horoscope being wrong for the first time ever, I somehow managed to sleep like a baby.

"HAPPY BIRTHDAY, BRYNN!" I heard. I blinked in the darkness and grabbed my phone. What? I looked around my bedroom, seeing no sunlight behind the blackout curtains. "Happy birthday, Brynn!" I heard again.

I threw my legs over my bed, confused. That's when I noticed my phone vibrating in my hand. My alarm. I looked down and saw a picture of Lindy from the bar last night, sticking out her tongue. She'd taken my purse with her during my embarrassing scuffle with Mr. Tall, Dark, and Handsome and must've taken a picture of herself.

"Happy birthday, Brynn!" my phone chirped again. I was going to kill Lindy for hijacking my phone with her overly cheerful wake-up call.

Though secretly I couldn't help but grin. Lindy had that effect on people.

I had the whole day to kill and had plans to meet my grandfather for brunch. First, I needed to get a bike ride in and then grab the largest coffee I could get my hands on. Two hours and thirty miles later, I hung my Specialized Allez Sprint on the wall of what was supposed to be my dining room. It now doubled as an at-home office and bike storage unit. Living in Dilworth had its perks, but the size of my townhouse wasn't one of them.

I'd grabbed a cup of joe from a neighborhood coffee shop rather than the big-named one that was closer. It tasted like dark-roasted heaven.

Lindy had already texted me twice, the first to say happy birthday again, and the second to remind me to grab my costume after brunch. I couldn't wait for the annual Heart Gala. It didn't always fall on my birthday, but the fundraiser always took place on the last weekend in October. It was the perfect time of year to don a costume and raise money for a good cause. Sterling and Masters was a platinum sponsor of the event, so regardless of whether I enjoyed it, I was expected to make an appearance—birthday or not.

I was all smiles by the time my Uber dropped me off in front of Paco's Taco and Tequila. I wouldn't be partaking in the tequila after last night, but I was craving their signature soft taco stuffed with chili-rubbed beef brisket, caramelized onions, cabbage, and my favorite chipotle barbecue sauce. It's what I ordered every year on my birthday with my grandfather. The more consistent I was around him, the more likely he was to remember me. I couldn't wait to see him. His episodes were getting worse, and soon, he wouldn't be able to live alone anymore—not even with the full-time nurse who stayed with him now.

"Brynnie!" he said, smiling. I released the breath I didn't know I was holding. His white hair was slicked back, and his bushy white mustache looked both dignified and up to no good all at once.

"Hi, Grampa," I said, sinking gratefully into his arms. I held on a moment too long, I knew that. But I never knew if the next time I was in his arms he would remember me.

He handed me a small box. "Happy birthday."

"What's this?" I asked, looking at the gold wrapping paper and vibrant autumn-hued bow. I waved hello to his nurse, Babs, who waited at the bar for us to finish lunch.

"Well, that would take all the fun out of it, now wouldn't it?" he said, his clear blue eyes twinkling as he laughed. He reached over the table with his arthritic hand. The blue veins were now prominent, but it was his wedding ring I focused on. Even after all this time alone, he never took it off. That was the kind of love I wanted some day.

"It's good to see you." I blinked back tears. It was too early, even for me, to get emotional.

"It's good to see you, too. Now open it! You don't want to make an old man wait. I might keel over before you get the wrapping paper off."

"Grampa!" I scolded. "That's not funny."

"Well, we all have to go sometime," he said with a cackle. "I'm not planning on it anytime soon, but I swear I've grown ten new white hairs waiting for you to open the dang box already."

I laughed, carefully sliding the bow from the box and setting the paper aside. It was silly, but I kept everything from him. He was the only family I had left, and I wanted to remember every moment with him.

He was right. We all had to go sometime. But I wasn't ready for it to be his turn yet. Not by a long shot.

My breath caught in my throat the moment I realized what was inside the box. "Grampa! No. I can't take this." I slid the box back across the table to him.

"Brynnie, hear me out," he said hoarsely. "Babs drives me everywhere these days. And I'm not allowed to drive anymore," he admitted.

"Oh, Grampa," I said, sighing. "When did that happen?"

"Last month. Was supposed to renew my license. Turns out you have to actually be able to see to drive. Who knew?" he teased.

"They're that bad?" I asked. His eyes had given him problems most of his adult life, but they'd gotten significantly worse over the years, and he wasn't a candidate for cataract surgery.

"Yep. But it's okay. I've got Babs. And when I don't anymore, when I'm in the old folks' home, I won't need to drive anyway. But you will. Because you'll need to come spring me from time to time," he said. He acted as if the upscale retirement community we'd already reserved for him was a prison cell.

I glanced down at the key to his baby—a burgundy Rolls-Royce convertible. It was too much. "Thank you, Grampa," I said, squeezing his hand. "I don't even know what to say."

"Thank you is enough. I know you'll take good care of her," he replied, clearing his throat. "I was hoping it would be a twofer celebration. You hear anything about that new job?"

"Unfortunately," I said. "They decided to go with an outsider. I won't get to meet the person till Monday."

"Now, why in tarnation would they do that?" he asked, chewing his carefully cut piece of burrito. "They had a perfectly qualified candidate internally."

"I don't know. I didn't exactly stick around to ask. I was too upset, and Carlisa sprang it on us late yesterday."

"Well, that was a crappy thing to do," he muttered. "People don't have any common sense these days."

"I agree," I said, laughing. "So, tell me about what's new in your world, Grampa. Is Miss Tulip Lady still giving you the googly eyes?"

He snickered. "She sure is. Haven't decided if I have enough energy to court her, though."

"Why not start with a simple hello?" I said gently.

He chuckled. "I don't have time these days to take things that slow, Brynn."

When we were done with lunch, he walked me to my "new" used car. I'd been planning to catch a ride home, but I had to admit as I looked down at the tan leather interior that it sure beat the back of another smelly Uber.

"She's gorgeous," I said, running my hand over the leather steering wheel. Even though it was over thirty years old, the Corniche was in mint condition with surprisingly few miles.

"Just like her new owner," he said as I climbed in. "Happy birthday, Brynnie."

I reached up and hugged him from inside the car. He must've had it detailed because it had that new car smell. "I love you, Grampa." I glanced over at Babs. "You call me if anything changes."

She nodded. "You know I will, honey."

"I'm right here, you know," Grampa grumbled as his nurse walked him to her car parked a few spots over.

"Say hi to Tulip Lady for me!" I called out before he climbed in. I could've sworn I heard Babs snicker.

Yesterday was epically shitty by all accounts. But, as I distanced myself from the mall traffic and hopped onto the highway to take the long way home, I had to admit it was shaping up to be much better today.

The warm Carolina sun washed over me as the wind picked up with my speed. I laughed in delight as my long hair whipped in my face, and I pressed the gas pedal.

Full acceleration ahead—birthday celebration, here I come!

CHAPTER FOUR

DESPITE MY LOVELY new wheels, I decided to catch an Uber to the Heart Gala. I knew I'd be drinking, especially after the doozy of a bombshell I got yesterday at work. And there was no way I was driving if I had a few drinks. Normally, I would've gone with Lindy, but Walter snagged that honor this year. I hated walking into events stag—especially on my birthday. I gnawed at the corner of my lip from my perch at the top of the stairs overlooking Founders Hall.

Below, the white, green, black, and gold marble floor twinkled and gleamed in its buffed perfection beneath the costumed feet of its guests. I glanced up at the tall, arched glass ceiling that covered the iconic two-story venue. The second floor, where I waited for Lindy, held a handful of closed shops around its perimeter. Guests coming in from the parking garage and other connected buildings brushed by me as they descended the marble stairs to join their friends and coworkers at the gala below.

The party was in full swing, and I couldn't wait to get down there. My foot tapped lightly against the marble as I pulled my cell phone from my black velvet clutch that was shaped like a raven. I would kill Lindy for making me wait so long alone.

"You know how to make quite an impression," a deep, sexy voice said from beside me. I turned slightly, my large black-feathered wings making it a challenge to maneuver easily. My eyes slid up the most magnificent specimen of a man's chest I'd ever laid eyes on, taking in the all-black ensemble. His dress shirt was unbuttoned indecently low, and a cape fell over a broad set of shoulders, tucked on one side behind a gleaming silver sword holstered at his hip. And, of course, he was wearing a signature black eye mask.

"Zorro, I presume?" I said, unable to meet the man's eyes, which were tucked away under the wide rim of his Bolero hat. He held out his gloved hand for mine. I went to shake it, and he surprised me by lifting my hand to his lips and kissing the back of it.

When the masked bandit lifted his gaze to meet mine, my heart nearly faltered in my chest. The eyes. They were a dark, magnificent blue. Familiar. It couldn't be. My gaze flicked to the man's wrist, but all I could see was where his poufy black sleeve met his black leather glove. I was being silly. Of course it wasn't the same man. What were the odds of that?

"The one and only," he said, bowing low at the waist. "Will I see you inside, my raven-haired beauty?"

I fought back the urge to roll my eyes, but there was something magnetic about the man—even with his cheesy lines and overly romantic gestures.

"You sure you're up for mingling with the Mistress of Evil?" I asked coyly.

He raked his eyes down my costume, from the twisted black horns to the matching skin-tight, torn dress that clung to my curves. I was Maleficent in all her dark glory.

"I'd like nothing more," he said.

I bit my lip and watched as he swished his cape and headed down the stairs.

He turned at the last moment. "Happy birthday, angel," he said, winking.

My jaw dropped, and I didn't have time to answer before Lindy's squeal from behind me nearly broke the sound barrier. I turned to see her shuffling toward me, as quickly as her tall red heels allowed.

"Oh my god!" I said, my eyes practically bulging from my head. I took in her thigh-high white stockings, her vibrant blue corset top, and the red leather crisscross straps that rose as if by magic from her cleavage.

She twirled in front of me. "Do you like it?"

Her flouncy, minuscule yellow skirt stood out to the sides straight, like a kid's too-small tutu that barely covered her butt. "You look hot as hell, my friend," I said.

I glanced over at Walter and chuckled at the way his steel gray eyes drank Lindy in beneath his dark, hooded robe. "Nice choice," I said to him with approval. He'd come as the wicked queen in her old hag disguise.

"I plan to corrupt her later with my poisoned apple," he said, cackling in full character.

Lindy affectionately rolled her eyes at Walter. "So, who was Tall, Dark, and Smoking Hot you were just talking to?" she asked as we descended the grand marble staircase.

She never missed a thing.

"I'm not sure, honestly. It's weird, but I get a feeling it's that same guy I ran into at Havana's last night. That's ridiculous, right?"

Lindy shrugged. "Not if he works in our building."

She had a point.

But before long, I lost track of Zorro in all the fun of the evening. We did a few too many shots to celebrate my twenty-eighth birthday—and to drown out the rage still eating at me over the loss of my job promotion. Before I knew it, I could hardly remember what he looked like, as Dan offered me a hand and twirled me out onto the dance floor. I'd long since had to abandon my black feathery wings because I'd hit one too many guests with them and was tired of apologizing.

"Lindy not available?" I joked as he spun me around and pulled me closer.

"I swear, one day she'll come to her senses," he muttered. I knew it was all in good fun. But I also knew he'd date her in a heartbeat if she ever asked. The poor guy just didn't have enough sense not to keep coming back for more punishment.

"You know, I think Shay has a thing for you—since you seem to be so masochistic."

Dan burst out laughing. "Nah—she's too tame for the likes of me."

Huh?

"Something you're not telling us, Dan? 'Cause I think she's the kind of woman who would pull a praying mantis on you, given the chance. She's not quite as squeaky clean as she pretends to be at work."

"Who knows, then? She might be right up my alley," he said, waggling his eyebrows. "Then again, I've done batshit crazy before. Ever dated a Sagittarius?" Dan shuddered.

I shook my head. "Can't say that I have. I'm a Scorpio," I said, as if that explained everything. When Dan's eyes furrowed down at me, I sighed. "Scorpio is a water sign, but most people mistake it for a fire sign because of the whole 'rise from the ashes' thing we're so good at. That, and we also tend to be stubborn, jealous, and hella passionate. We're awfully fiery for a water sign, so we don't do well with other fire signs."

"I didn't even know Sagittarius *was* a fire sign," he said, chuckling. "Makes sense though now that I think about it. Hmm . . . I wonder what sign Shay is."

"Dan!" I said and rolled my eyes. "She's the sign of the devil. That's what sign she is."

We were laughing and having a good time when Lindy interrupted us on the dance floor to say goodbye. I couldn't help but see the open longing in Dan's eyes as he appreciated her costume.

"Sure you don't want a prince instead?" he asked Lindy, running a hand over his own costume. I had to admit, he did look awfully cute in his Prince Florian costume with its red cape.

Lindy mock-punched Dan in the arm, then turned to me instead of answering our coworker. "I'm sorry, but we have to split," she practically yelled in my ear so I could hear her over the loud music. The DJ had cranked up the tunes and started playing something considerably sexier. It must have been that time of night.

"But it's my birthday!" I hollered back.

"I know! I'm sorry. It's getting late, and we have a long drive back to the lake."

I rolled my eyes. I'd forgotten she was staying at Walter's house on Lake Norman tonight. "Fine!" I said dramatically.

"But call me in the morning. Maybe we can go for a run or get our toes done?"

"I'd love to!" she agreed, giving me a big hug before taking off.

I was about to tell Dan I should probably get going too when someone tapped my shoulder. "May I grab a dance with the birthday girl?"

I looked up, and there they were again. Those fucking sapphire eyes that made my panties melt practically right off me. Sometimes the passionate Scorpio got the best of me. I couldn't help but lower my eyes and flush pink under his intense gaze.

It didn't take long for Dan to take the hint and bow out, ever the gentleman.

I offered the dark, handsome rogue in front of me my hand, and he pulled me close so we could sway to the fun, sexy tune being crooned by Charlie Puth and Meghan Trainor. I sucked in a quick breath of air, my heartrate accelerating faster than it had a right to with a stranger. I had so many questions I wanted to ask, but my body took over when he pressed his hips against mine, rolling them in perfect harmony with the music. He rested his hands on my hips possessively, and I'd never felt sexier than I did under the heated intensity of his gaze.

The man was a freaking sex magnet.

He smirked, his blue eyes twinkling as he took my hand and spun me in a circle. When I came back front and center, he surprised me. His large, strong hand supported my lower back, and the next thing I knew, he was dipping me—a perfect ending to the sexy little number we were dancing to. It was like we were in a movie. I couldn't look away from his eyes, and I couldn't hear the next song that came on. I knew people were still dancing around us somewhere, but all I could see was this man.

This gorgeous, sinfully hot man.

Fuck it.

It was my birthday. My friends just left me. And I was getting a birthday kiss at the very least. I stood on my tiptoes and wrapped my hands around his neck, the intent clear in my eyes as I stared at his full red lips. It was bold, but I was tired of the games. Like the song said, I was ready to get it on.

But my mystery masked Zorro didn't let me. He reached his hand up behind my head and gripped my hair all sexy as fuck, pulling my head back and forcing me to look up at him. That's when I realized he was discreetly walking me backward, off the dance floor. I was in a freaking trance, my eyes unable to look away or care what anyone else might've thought.

He kept leading me until my bare back hit a cold marble wall. We were in a private alcove off the main dance floor. My chest rose and fell in anticipation of a kiss. We'd only said a few words to each other all night, but there was something so magnetic about my dark and handsome stranger that drew me to him, made me crave the taste of him. I couldn't fight it if I wanted to.

It was that, or all the drinks I'd had.

"Are you going to tease me all night, or finally kiss me?"

"You're bold, birthday girl."

"No, I'm curious," I said, wetting my lips. I reached up and pulled his hat off, then lifted his eye mask. Sure enough, the same man I'd run into at Havana's stared back at me, sweat beading his brow from our time on the crowded dance floor. "It *is* you."

"We meet again," he said playfully. "You weren't so curious last night."

I leaned into him. "I'm curious now."

"So you are," he said, gripping my hair tighter. Lust shot straight to my core, setting my insides on fire.

Calm the fuck down, I told myself. *Just take your kiss and go home.*

Before I had a chance to consider the wisdom of my boldness, his mouth crashed down onto mine. Like the night before, his lips were soft but firm. Commanding. It was as if he owned me already and knew exactly how he wanted to taste me. His warm, thick tongue passed over my lips, pressing forward as he pulled me closer to his mouth. I may've whimpered, lifting my hands to his face as he explored my mouth. I shamelessly nearly climbed the man, my legs desperately aching to get closer. I was letting this stranger practically fuck me with his tongue, and I didn't care who saw us. This was hands down the most wickedly sinful kiss I'd ever had—and I'd had my fair share.

His mouth was hot, and he tasted like sex on a stick. And I wanted it. In fact, I wanted more. I ran my hands up the back of his head, through his thick dark brown hair. My nipples responded when he playfully bit my lower lip.

"Curious for even more?" he growled quietly into my ear.

I knew what he meant. He'd made it clear last night when he'd handed me his room key. I knew if I went with him, it would be nothing short of explosive. But he was a stranger, and I couldn't be *that* careless—no matter how badly I wanted to get laid on my birthday.

"I am," I said hesitantly.

"But?" he asked, his forehead pressed against mine as our chests rose and fell together in sync.

"I don't even know your real name, Casanova," I pointed out, using the endearment Lindy had knighted him with the evening before.

"Pierce," he growled, leaning in and kissing my throat. His tongue slid warm against my skin, making my panties wetter by the second. "Does it really matter?" he asked, his hand finding my side and pulling me closer to the solid wall of his abs.

I swallowed. Did it? Should it? I'd never had a full-on one-night stand with a stranger before. I'd always known the person through a friend or colleague. But I had to admit, I was far past simple curiosity. There was a strange connection pulling me toward this man, and it had already morphed into a straight-up, hard-core longing that I knew I wouldn't be able to walk away from without regret.

Hell, you're only twenty-eight once.

"Give me your driver's license," I said.

"Excuse me?"

"Your driver's license. I'm not getting in a car with a complete stranger on my birthday without someone knowing where I am. That's how women end up in little pieces in some guy's refrigerator."

He quirked his eyebrow at me, a smirk lifting the corner of his mouth. "Well, we wouldn't want that now, would we?"

He pulled out his driver's license and handed it to me. Pierce Abrams. That sounded nice and normal, right? New York City. So, he *was* just visiting. Good. I wouldn't have to run into him again and be mortified. I could do this, right? Lots of women did.

I took a picture of his license and texted it to Lindy.

This is Mr. Tall, Dark, and Handsome. And I have every intention of going back to the Lion's Den with Casanova tonight. I'll text you on my way home later.

I immediately got a text back.

Holy fuck! He's even hotter than I remember. You go, girl! Make him wear a condom! We don't know where Zorro's sword has been.

I burst out laughing.

"You checked out," I said, kissing his mouth again and tugging at his lower lip with my teeth. "Let me just grab my wings, and we can go."

He growled into my mouth and cupped my breast, running his thumb over the thin fabric. "Leave them here."

"I can't. I rented them."

He swore under his breath. "Fine. Get your wings, angel. I'll let my driver know."

His driver?

We grabbed my wings and headed toward the stairs, his hand firmly holding mine as he spoke quickly into his phone. Five minutes later, after we'd wound our way through a maze of closed overstreet walkways, we emptied out into a parking deck, where a black sedan waited for us. A man in a three-piece suit stepped out and nodded before taking my giant wings from me. I watched as he folded them gracefully into the trunk. Satisfied, I slid inside the back of the town car and waited as Pierce spoke quietly to his driver, then climbed in beside me.

The minute the door closed, Pierce pressed a button, and a partition slid up between us and the driver. Then, his mouth descended on mine again. I let him in, swallowing his kisses as he pressed me back against the buttery soft leather interior. I pressed my hips up, needing to feel his body even closer. It was like a fuse was lit the moment we were alone. I couldn't imagine what would happen when we had complete privacy.

"You never told me your name, birthday girl," he said, his voice husky with need as he ran his hands over my chest.

My head fell back against the seat. How did he expect me to remember my name when his tongue was doing deliciously naughty things along my throat and collarbone?

"Brynn," I choked out, my breath catching when his hand slid over the top of my thigh, close to my core.

"Does birthday girl have a last name? Maybe I should send my driver a picture of your license?" he teased.

"Hartley," I said. Why did him having my full name suddenly feel vulnerable when I was about to go do very naughty things with this stranger? And when he'd given me his information so willingly?

"Brynn Hartley," he said, his eyes roaming over me as if memorizing my every curve. "It suits you."

I bit my lip, my arms breaking out in goose bumps as his fingers trailed between my thighs and lightly brushed the skin there. I didn't have time to reply though because the car suddenly came to a stop. I glanced out the window and saw the shiny gold and glass exterior of the Lion's Den hotel. I'd been there before for work events, but never to stay the night. Not that I was staying the night, I mean. I was sure I'd be gone within the hour.

My mind was running a thousand miles a minute as we rode the elevator to the top floor, his thumb tracing circles on the back of my hand. "Get out of your head, birthday girl."

The elevator opened, and we exited right into the penthouse suite. Holy shit. This man had money. And a lot of it. But I didn't have long to admire the room before I felt his strong hands wrap around my waist. We stood at the window and looked out at the twinkling Queen City in front of us. I could easily see the Corporate Center where we'd just danced at Founders Hall—it was the tallest building in Charlotte.

My head fell back against his chest, and I closed my eyes. His hands roamed my body, his mouth burning hot against the flesh of my neck. I'd unequivocally never wanted another man so badly in my entire life. I pressed my backside against him, eliciting a groan from Pierce as he cupped my breasts and squeezed. His fingers skillfully kneaded the hard buds of my nipples, and there was no hiding how aroused I was.

"I don't normally do this," I whispered. I don't know why I said it, but I felt like I needed to before we went any further.

Every cell in my body wanted what was about to come.

"We don't have to," he said gruffly, the kick of his dick against my back telling me he was ready when I was, though. "But I want you, Brynn Hartley. I wanted you from the moment I saw you last night at Havana's."

I turned in his arms, my insides going soft at his words.

"I don't know what it is about you," I said, glancing into those hypnotic blue eyes of his. "But I'm past curious."

I reached down and stroked him through his pants. "It's my birthday, right?"

"That it is, angel." He led me toward the bedroom, then kicked the door closed and shrugged out of his cape. His eyes told me everything I needed to know. "And the birthday girl gets anything she wants tonight," he said, pulling me into his arms.

"In that case . . ."

CHAPTER FIVE

WE FUCKED SO hard and fast the first time, I never even had a chance to take off my dress or my horns. I didn't care that they bounced on my head as he slammed into me over and over again, bent over the bedframe in the hotel's master suite. It was hot, sweaty, and sinful as fuck.

I was swollen and bruised and thirsty for more when I felt him slide out of me, squeezing my backside. It was my fault really. We'd barely gotten the door closed when I pulled his thick shaft from his pants. It was my birthday after all, right? And I'd wanted him between my thighs stat. I was soaked from the anticipation all night—and sometimes, when you're a little too tipsy and horny, you just need it hard and fast.

And boy did Casanova live up to his name and deliver.

"I guess you were able to keep up with the Mistress of Evil after all," I said with a laugh, my thighs still shaking.

"We haven't even started yet," he snarled, spinning me around to face him.

He gripped my upper arms and yanked me closer, his mouth consuming mine with even more heat than before.

It was like he'd gotten a taste of me and needed more. I knew the feeling. I unbuttoned his white dress shirt and clenched my thighs when his chiseled chest and perfect abs came into view.

Thank you, Jesus!

Forget Casanova. This man was Adonis in the flesh. Dark hair lightly peppered his chest and trailed down his stomach. His pants were unzipped, and his cock was still encased in the condom I'd made sure he put on.

He was enormous—my swollen insides were testament to that. All I could think about was having him inside of me again.

"Let's clean up," he said, as if reading my mind. "I want your legs around my head in the next five minutes."

Fuck.

"If you insist," I said with a laugh. I lowered my Maleficent dress over my ass and removed my horns, setting them on the table next to the bed as I made my way to the bathroom.

"Those were fucking hot," he said, following closely behind me. "I have to say—that was definitely a first."

I chucked. "For me too." I turned the water on in the shower and looked over my shoulder at him. "Do you mind if I clean up before I go home?"

He stormed across the bathroom and lifted my chin as the hot water steamed up the room around us. "You're not sneaking off yet. I wasn't kidding when I said I wasn't done with you. I think you and I both know there's a lot more left to burn off between us than a fast ten-minute fuck."

I swallowed. He was right. And god, I wanted more.

"I'm going to devour every inch of your body tonight, birthday girl. Then fuck you so hard you'll remember the feeling of me inside you for the next week."

Christ! Who was this man, and where in the world had he come from?

Oh, right. New York, I chuckled to myself.

"Then get undressed already, and let's go," I challenged him. Confidence had never been an issue for me.

I slowly peeled my dress off my five-eight frame and watched in delight as his eyes assessed my long, lean body. I was a cyclist and did yoga at least twice a week. I was probably in the best shape of my life. My abs weren't quite the marbled work of art his were, but they were flat and hard when I flexed them. It was my ass, though, that made his eyes cloud over with unbridled lust. He ran his tongue over his lower lip and bit it. Then he dropped his pants and shrugged off his shirt in a hurry, pressing me forward into the large open shower.

I noticed he had a thing about leading, and it was kind of hot. I was usually the sexual aggressor in a relationship—confident in both who I was and what I wanted. But Pierce was next-level assertive. I'd never really been with someone like him before, but I was willing to let go of control for once and let myself just be *taken* by this man.

He wanted to devour me? Be my fucking guest!

He pressed me up against the cool tiled wall. Hot water slid over my body as Pierce picked up a washcloth, slathered it with body wash, and then slid it firmly between my thighs. The hard arch of his hand and thumb pressed up into my wet center. I wantonly slid my hips back and forth as he washed me. I needed some part of him back inside me fast.

Anything.

He pulled one of the many shower heads from its holder on the wall and turned it, aiming its spray straight up inside me until all the soap was gone and my clit was throbbing with need. He gripped my chin as the spray assaulted my sensitive nub, then he ran his thick, wet tongue over my lips—my mouth greedy for the taste of him again. His tongue danced with mine as he brought the spray even closer. My thighs shook as his tongue plunged deeper inside my mouth, my head held captive by his tight grip. Right when I didn't think I could take it another second, he hung the shower head back up, then dropped to his knees in front of me.

Holy hell. If I thought the man was hot before, he was a full-fledged god now.

Water streamed over his dark hair as he pulled my hips forward and tossed my leg over his shoulder. Without warning, he lowered his head and buried his face against my pussy.

Fuck!

Fuck! Fuck! Fuckity fuck!

His tongue sliced through my wet opening and plunged deep inside me. My legs shook as he alternated from biting and sucking my clit to pressing his face between my thighs to work me over with his tongue. It soothed the ache momentarily, then his teeth brought delicious torture to my core again as he rolled my sensitive nub back and forth. I was so close to combusting by the time he finally drove his fingers deep inside me. He held me there, at his mercy and on the brink, until he slowly curled them, beckoning my orgasm from me until my thighs shook and I could barely stand.

His fingers slowed but stayed where they were, milking every last spasm from my body. My body rocked with his, my eyes closed from the overwhelming ecstasy still flooding through my burning core. I wanted to return the favor—I needed to taste him. But before I could open my eyes, he stood and pressed the thick head of his cock at my entrance.

"We—we need a condom," I said, my breath shaking and uneven with need.

"Just once," he said. "Let me slide inside you, Brynn. I want to feel your tight pussy wrapped around me."

My body screamed yes, but somewhere deep inside, my level head said, *Wait. We don't even really know him.*

I couldn't. As much as I wanted to feel him bareback—right this second!—I didn't know his sexual history.

"I can't," I said, worried that he would tell me to get out then. But it wasn't something I was willing to budge on, not even for another life-shattering orgasm from my sinfully addictive, dark-haired Casanova.

He nodded, lowering his head and nibbling my lip instead.

"Couldn't hurt to ask," he said with a chuckle. Then he took my hand and led me out of the shower. We didn't even dry off. He led me back to the bedroom and playfully shoved me onto the bed, dutifully grabbing a condom from the bedside table. "What's your favorite position, birthday girl?"

"On my stomach," I admitted breathily. "But I'm kinda liking the view from right here." I admired his swollen cock as he slowly rolled the condom down its impressive length.

"Prone it is," he said gruffly, making me squeal when he flipped me over. I hardly had time to catch my breath when he pressed his tip inside me from behind. My body was flat against the bed, and Pierce was holding himself up over me. I felt the first long, thick stroke of his cock as he pressed all the way deep inside me.

"Oh god," I moaned. He was buried to the hilt, and my walls ached as they stretched to accommodate him. He leaned down and bit my shoulder, my ass rising to meet each thrust of his hips. My body bounced against the bed every delicious time he slammed inside me. My nipples were on fire from rubbing against the comforter, and it was causing my clit to flare with the stimulation. I was somewhere in outer space, lost in oblivion, as I let Pierce take over and drill into me over and over again. I swear, I was having an out-of-body experience he was fucking me for so long. I gripped the bedding, my body wracking with spasms as wave after wave of another torrential orgasm finally flooded through me.

"Holy fuck!" I cried out, pressing my face into the mattress.

I knew he still needed to come, though. Before I had time to recover, Pierce shifted, grabbing my hips as he lowered to his knees. He pulled my ass closer, then dipped his finger down between my cheeks and wet his thumb, running it along my open slit where my vaginal walls clenched around his thick shaft.

I could feel him looking at where our bodies met and wished I could see what he was looking at as he slid back and forth inside me, so torturously slow now. Then he gently rolled his thumb over the tight, puckered hole of my backside, pressing it gently. I knew what he was asking, and my insides burned at the heated animalistic need that rushed over me. I pressed my ass back, letting him push his thumb inside me.

"Fuck, Brynn," he said, his voice thick with raw desire.

He set a delicious, toe-curling pace, rocking his hips back and forth as his thumb slowly stroked inside my ass and made my entire body drip with need again. When neither of us could stand it anymore, he let his thumb slide out before gripping my arms and pulling me all the way up until my back was flush against his chest.

My body panted for the drilling that I knew was coming when he drove his cock straight up inside me, my body bucking off his hips. "God, Pierce!" I screamed out.

"Come with me," he grit out between clenched teeth.

It wasn't hard to give in to his demand. I was drenched, aroused even further from the unexpected ass play and solid fuck. I lowered my hand and furiously rubbed my clit as he relentlessly thrust himself inside me. It didn't take long for his deep penetration to send me skyrocketing again—and just in time.

"Fuck," he howled, burying himself as deeply as he could as he arched back. I felt torrents of his hot come pour into the condom, his cock bouncing with the release. My thighs were shaking, totally spent, by the time he was done coming and lowered my chest back to the bed.

He grunted as he rolled off me and onto his back. Pierce threw an arm over his face and laughed, then wrapped an arm over my sweaty back and kissed the same shoulder he'd bitten earlier. "Jesus fucking Christ, Brynn," he said low.

I laughed into the comforter. No other words were needed.

I knew exactly what he meant.

My body was spent, used, swollen, satiated, and decimated—all at once.

He'd consumed every inch of me.

And still, I wanted more.

CHAPTER SIX

WE ORDERED ROOM service and sat naked on the bed, eating hot, salty french fries, flatbread pizza, and a decadent slice of seven-layer cake. What can I say? When you're still slightly tipsy, and you just burned off thousands of calories, you'll eat most anything.

Pierce even had room service put a candle in the cake and told me to make a wish. I was certain it was about to come true when I looked over, his eyes darkening as he watched me lick the frosting from my fork. I gasped, laughter bubbling over, when he dipped his fingers into the top of the cake and pressed me back against the bed. My eyes were transfixed on his as he grinned up at me, something wicked brewing behind his dark lashes.

"Spread your legs for me, Brynn," he said quietly.

I licked my lips as I looked down at him. I'd never been the submissive sort, but I swear there was something about this man that made me want to throw away every inhibition and debase myself for him. I slowly opened my thighs.

I gasped when his fingers messily spread the cold frosting over the outside of my pussy. He winked, getting comfortable on his stomach before burying his face between my thighs and licking the sticky, sweet sugar from my lips. I laughed until he bit my thigh, then yanked me down the bed till I was under him. "You're the best thing I've had to eat all weekend," he said.

"I'd like to know the feeling too," I said. I reached over and stuck my fingers in the cake. "Stand up."

Understanding flashed over his eyes, making them even smokier and more intense. He didn't waste any time standing at the foot of the bed. I crawled my way down and wrapped my chocolate-coated hand around his thick shaft. Pierce hissed when I wrapped my lips around the tip of his swollen cock and slowly kissed him.

Between the chocolate and the musky scent of sexy, raw Pierce, I wanted to pass out I was so aroused. He tasted like heaven, with or without the sticky confectionary sugar. Chocolate was everywhere as I used my hand to stroke him while bobbing my head down his long shaft. He held my head, thrusting his hips as we found our pace together, my tongue swirling around him with every pass of my lips. There was just no way that I could take him all the way in my mouth at this angle, so I pulled my head back, my eyes meeting his. His gaze was unfocused, clouded over thick with desire as he watched my mouth move slowly off his shaft.

I rolled onto my back and looked up at him, his heavy cock bobbing over my head. "Come here," I said. He started walking around the side of the bed, mistaking the change in my position. I grabbed his hand, forcing him to stop. He looked down at me, stroking my hair to the side as I gathered my courage to tell him what I really wanted.

"No," I said, my voice raspy with desire. "I want you to fuck my mouth—like this," I said, pulling his hand so he was standing at my head again, above me. "I want to taste all of you, Pierce."

His head dropped back, and he groaned. But Pierce slowly started stroking himself with his other hand. "You sure about this?"

I nodded and pulled him closer by his thighs. I let my head fall over the end of the bed and guided the swollen head of his cock back to my lips. It was the only way I could think of to take him all the way in. I'd give it the old college try, at least.

"Fuck," he said, gripping the sides of my head as he slowly fed his cock into my throat from above like I'd asked. I held onto his thighs and let him set the pace, my breasts bouncing as he pumped slowly into my mouth. He never gave me more than I could hold, but I was able to taste far more of him this way and loved the feel of him pressing deep inside the back of my throat.

Pierce arched over my body, his hips finding a steady, comfortable pace as he slid his fingers over my mons and back inside my wet center. I moaned against his cock, arching my hips to invite his fingers in even deeper. It was as if, no matter how much of him I got, I simply couldn't get enough—even though he was still a stranger to me. Maybe *because* he was a stranger. I felt completely uninhibited and without shame as instinct took over and desire ruled my body.

For just one night, I could give. Take. Explore. Push my boundaries.

He'd shown me he was respectful of my needs, while willing to take any inch I gave.

I knew I might not have another chance to truly let go like this. Pierce was my birthday wish come true, and I was going to go to the very brink with this man. I knew it in my core. One night of no-holds-barred, carnal fucking. I'd let him use me. I'd use him. Then I'd kiss him goodbye and have fantasy fuel for the next six months—since my heart was still bruised after Nick, and prospects were pretty dried up in my world these days.

"Fuck, Brynn, you need to stop," he growled, though his hands found the sides of my face and he pressed his cock even deeper into my throat. I felt him pulse, on the brink of coming. I wanted to taste more than the few little droplets that were on the tip of his cock when he'd pressed past my lips that first, glorious time. But I couldn't.

I pulled my head back, cupping his balls in my hand. "Come on my stomach," I said.

He gripped his cock, yanking it a few times as I lifted my head and licked along the bottom of his sac. It pushed him over the edge, his legs tensing as he released onto my stomach with an animalistic growl.

I ran my hands over the warm, thick liquid, rubbing it in as I kissed the delicate skin between his thighs, his body jerking at the little flicks of my tongue. He reached his hand down, stroking his fingers through my hair as he gazed at me, reverently almost.

"Up," he murmured.

I rolled over onto my stomach and pressed off the bed. He yanked off the soiled comforter and tossed it to the floor, then took my hand and led me to an alcove in the master suite. It had a separate set of tinted glass doors I hadn't noticed, made to look like a walk-in closet. I gasped when he opened them, realizing it was a fully equipped cedarwood sauna. The rich almost-red wood practically vibrated with energy as steam rose from the hot black rocks to the side.

Pierce opened a small chest and took out a warm wash-cloth, rubbing it over my belly. He used another one to clean off his shaft, as there was still chocolate frosting around the base. We both laughed when we looked at each other, finding lingering bits of frosting on the corners of our mouths and on our fingers. He leaned forward, pressing two of his fingers into my mouth so I could clean the frosting off. Then he dipped his head and licked the side of my mouth. For some reason, the tender, intimate move nearly decimated me.

I was holding my breath, my heart hammering inside my chest, when he turned me around so I could get a view of the city beyond the large tinted window. I took his hand and led him to the bench along the wall in front of it. He wrapped his arms around my waist and put his chin on my shoulder as we looked out at the twinkling lights.

"What's that building over there?" he asked, pointing at the bright pink, neon glow coming from one of the office buildings in the distance.

"That's the Duke Energy corporate office," I said. "They light it up different colors for different events. This month is breast cancer awareness month, so it's bright pink."

"That's beautiful," he said. He brushed my hair off my shoulder as he began sucking the skin. It didn't take long for my flesh to pebble again. "I can't stop wanting you, Brynn."

"I know," I whispered.

"I keep telling myself after the next time, we'll talk some more. I'll let the poor woman rest. Then, I see your naked body, and I crave the fucking taste of you."

I nodded, leaning my head back against his chest as he reached his hands around and cupped my breasts. He rolled the nipples gently, then applied more pressure and pinched them. I moaned, pressing my thighs together.

"Have you ever worn nipple clamps before?" he asked huskily.

I nodded, my bottom pressing back at the thought.

"Who for?"

"Myself," I said. "I've never worn them with a lover, but I have a pair. I wear them sometimes when I masturbate."

He groaned against my neck, pinching my nipples harder. "What I wouldn't do to have a pair right now," he said. He turned me around in his arms, then dipped his head. "Your tits are fucking perfect."

He lapped his tongue over a nipple, grinning when my body spasmed at the soft flick he lashed me with next. "Your nipples are so sensitive," he murmured, popping one all the way into his mouth.

My back arched, and I reached out, grabbing his head. I held him tight to my chest as he sucked hard on my delicate flesh. I was getting wetter again by the second. I swear I was about to come just from his tongue against my pebbled nipple. He popped it out of his mouth and stood up.

"Wait here," he said mysteriously.

I bit my lip, having no clue what he was up to. I stared out at the Queen City in the distance. How the hell had I wound up at the Lion's Den, in a sauna overlooking the city, on my birthday? Correction—it was no longer my birthday. It was Halloween now. And though I had no solid plans, I wanted time with Lindy today to tell her everything. I needed time to let my body recover from my endless rounds of hot sex with Pierce. And even though I'd promised myself no work this weekend, there were always emails I could answer, and my house wasn't going to clean itself.

My mind was clearing up, and my day-to-day life was threatening to slip back in just as Pierce returned to the sauna.

"No deep thoughts," he said, kissing my throat. "Only pleasure tonight."

My body instantly responded to Pierce's lips, his warm tongue.

"Close your eyes," he said.

I turned my head to look at him, searching his intense gaze.

"Do you trust me?" he asked.

His eyes were piercing blue, and for some reason, I felt as if they broke through every barrier of mine until they reached the rawest depths of my soul. It was beyond unnerving, especially since Pierce was virtually a stranger to me.

Did I trust him?

I was in his hotel room, wasn't I?

"I do," I whispered.

"Good. Now close your eyes, birthday girl. I have a little surprise for you."

I looked out at the city one last time before closing my eyes. Cool silk brushed my skin as Pierce secured a blindfold around my eyes, driving my world into complete darkness.

CHAPTER SEVEN

THE TIE WASN'T too tight, and the cool, silky fabric made my thighs tingle with anticipation. I'd only let one other boyfriend tie me up or practice any light BDSM-type sex play in the bedroom—and he'd been my boyfriend for close to three years. So, the fact that I was handing over complete control to a near stranger told me I might be a little too far gone on the sex-crazed scale tonight.

He ran his hands over my shoulders and down my arms. Goose bumps broke out over my skin. "God, do you have any idea how beautiful you are?" he asked, trailing kisses down my back. My chest was heaving with anticipation from not being able to see or know what was coming next.

Pierce cupped my ass, lifting it in his hands and kissing it. Then, he drew in a mouthful of flesh and sucked so hard I knew I'd have a bruise there tomorrow. He massaged my cheeks as he sucked my flesh, making me wetter than I imagined I'd feel from such a simple act.

When he stood, I felt the long, thick rod of his shaft press against me as he leaned in and kissed my neck and ears again. I shivered.

"Have you ever given up control, Brynn?"

I shook my head.

"Do you want to?"

I bit my lip, unsure.

He placed his hand between my thighs from behind and slid his finger back and forth over my wet slit. He chuckled. "You do, baby girl," he said. "Whether you know it or not, you do."

I nodded, my heart hammering.

"For the rest of our time together, you will do as I say."

I swallowed. Could I really do this? What if he asked me to do something I didn't want to? I suppose I wouldn't be here that much longer anyway. How hard could it be to let him be a little bossy in the bedroom for the rest of the night?

"Are we clear?"

I nodded.

"I won't do anything you're uncomfortable with, but I want to push you, Brynn. Your body was made for me to fuck, to play with, to dominate."

Holy shit. Why was I getting so wet with each slow, deliberate word he was saying?

"I want every minute I can get with you while I'm here—do you understand?"

It was just one night, right? So sure. Why not.

"Yes, sir," I said, unsure if I was saying or doing the right thing.

"I'm not a dom, Brynn," he said. "You don't have to call me sir."

I swallowed. "What if I want to?"

He chuckled. "If it turns you on, you can call me anything you want to."

I licked my lips, my pussy clenching.

Pierce gathered both of my hands behind my back and wrapped another tie around them, binding them together. They settled nicely just above my ass. I couldn't help it. I had to full-on bite my lip from moaning at the idea of being blindfolded and tied up in front of him. Lindy was going to lose her shit when I told her—though I was quite sure she and Walter did this kind of stuff all the time. She told me once that she called him Daddy in the bedroom.

There was no way I was calling Pierce that.

He turned me around, then said, "Take a deep breath in, then hold it. Don't release it until I tell you to."

I did as he said, though not sure why. As soon as I got to the top of my inhalation, I nearly cried out. Something cold and metal bit into the flesh of my nipple, squeezing it hard. I whimpered, my body nearly buckling. Then I felt the cold pinch on my other nipple. They both burned, the fire striking a trail of need right from my nipples to my thighs.

Pierce cupped both of my breasts in his hands and kneaded them, giving me some relief. "Release your breath now, Brynn."

I exhaled, my body shaking under his gaze. I couldn't see him, but I could *feel* his eyes on me.

"I thought you didn't have any nipple clamps."

His hands roamed down my sides, then found my hot, ready sex. He gripped my thighs tightly. "I improvised," he said. Then he guided me by the shoulders to have a seat on the warm wood slats of the bench. "There are lots of things at hand if you get a little creative."

Between the heat and my arousal, I was having a hard time breathing. Little beads of sweat gathered at my hair line as I imagined what he had clamped down over my nipples.

"You're so fucking perfect," he murmured.

I whimpered.

He gently pulled at one of the metal clamps and lifted, shooting heat straight to my core. I drew in a shaky, gasping breath and heard Pierce chuckle.

"You like that?"

"Yes," I admitted.

He tugged the other, both nipples now taut with tension. I moaned out loud, biting my lip from the exquisite pain.

Then I felt his fingers part my thighs, playing lightly with the small smattering of hair down there, where I kept a close, natural shave. He rolled his thumb over my swollen clit, my thighs shaking with each pass. Then his warm mouth closed over it, drawing it in so deep I gasped, wanting to reach for his thick head of hair so I could rock my core against his mouth.

But my hands were tied.

Sweet Jesus.

He worked me over with his mouth as two fingers slid deep inside me, forcing my bottom off the bench as I arched toward the only thing bringing me relief: his tongue. I could hear the steam sizzling off the hot rocks. I could smell the scent of my arousal. But most of all, I could feel the way my body was on high alert—anticipating the next delicious surprise.

As he fucked me with his fingers, he guided me to stand, then turned me around. I whimpered when he tugged at my nipples again, my eyes rolling back beneath his tie.

Then he pressed the swollen tip of his cock against the entrance of my pussy, dipping the tip in and getting it wet, then pulling it out before dipping the tip back in.

"Squeeze your legs tight together for me, baby girl," he said, his breath warm against my ear. I shivered, closing my thighs tightly. He pushed his thick cock between my thighs and let it rub along the outside of my pussy until it hit my clit. He rubbed it like this a few times back and forth till we were both sopping wet with my juices.

Then he spread open my cheeks and guided the tip of his cock to my ass. "Have you ever been taken like this, Brynn?"

I shook my head. I'd done many adventurous things before, but that wasn't one of them. I wasn't exactly opposed. The situation had just never arisen before.

He pressed his tip forward gently, and I felt the ache of both need and pain that was about to explode around me if I let him.

"May I?" he asked, licking his tongue up my sweaty back to my collarbone. He suckled on the skin, gently pressing with the tip of his cock at my entrance. He was soaked with my desire, and quite frankly, I was curious.

"Yes, sir," I said. It felt right somehow. He was, after all, staking claim to every inch of my body tonight in a way I'd never let another.

"Fuck," he growled.

He pushed the tip of his dick all the way in. I moaned, pressing back against him.

"Do you have a condom on?" I asked.

"I do, baby girl." He pistoned his hips to let me get used to the feel of just his head inside me. "There's no way this isn't going to hurt at first, but it'll give way to exquisite pleasure soon enough, okay?"

I nodded, eager for the burn that was coming.

He reached around, unclasping whatever was on my nipples. The pain of them coming off almost hurt worse than the tension of having them on. My nipples ached. As he massaged my tits and rubbed my nipples back to life, he pressed his cock deeper, deeper until I couldn't hold back anymore.

I screamed out as he pressed all the way in, the gentle skin stretching to accommodate his girth. "Fuck!" I hissed, my ass clenching around him as he continued to squeeze my tits.

He stayed that way for a minute to let me adjust. I had to admit, it was better that way. I was so focused on his hands that the pressure of him burying himself deep inside my ass didn't last as long as it could have.

I couldn't believe I was letting Pierce do this to me. I took a deep breath, my thighs shaking.

"Hey, are you okay?" he asked.

I nodded, trying to be braver than I felt. But shit! It *hurt.*

"You're just—bigger than I expected," I said, laughing shakily.

"You'll adjust, trust me," he coaxed. "But if it hurts too much, we can stop. I'll be just as happy buried inside your tight little pussy."

Christ! The way he talked to me was enough to bring me to my edge. "No," I said. "I want you to keep going. I want to see it all the way through."

His laughter rolled over my skin in warm, rich waves, setting off micro-explosions along my body. "As you wish, birthday girl."

He gripped my bound wrists and slowly stroked back and forth inside me. He was so big and so thick. It felt like there wasn't a single ounce of space left. But slowly, slowly, my body relaxed, and we fell into a pleasurable rhythm that indeed was bringing me exquisite pleasure I never imagined possible from this.

"Fuck, Brynn," he said, holding on to my ass as he drove himself in and out.

Pleasure tore through me as I climaxed, my muscles contracting around his cock. "Oh my god," I cried out as his hips thrust faster. "Pierce!"

"Yeah, baby?"

My thighs were now shaking as pleasure shot through me. "Oh my god . . . I didn't know I could come like this. Fuck!"

He chuckled, reaching around and squeezing my breasts again as he powered through. He drove his hips fast and hard as he chased his own climax. It didn't take long for me to feel his cock pulse before warm, thick currents shot inside of me. I wish I could've felt it without the condom. I was on the pill, and it was anal, so I wasn't worried about that obviously. It was simply the unknown—with someone unknown.

My body shook around him as he held still, his cock bouncing as the last drops filled his condom inside me. Then he slowly eased out, my backside on fire.

He pulled me onto his lap in the sauna, and we sat there together, breathing shallow from the exertion and the heat. We were covered in sweat, and the small room reeked of our passion. My body was exhausted, spent from a night of pure, delicious debauchery. I'd never been more sexually satiated, though, and a small smile spread over my face.

Pierce picked me up in his arms and carried me to the bathroom, where he stood me up in the shower. The blindfold was still on, and I could hardly stand, my body was so worn and well loved. But the cool spray was sweet relief on my skin. He washed my body, my hair, my thighs. He dropped warm, tender kisses over each part where I suspected I'd have bruises later. Then I heard him quickly wash himself before turning off the water and wrapping me in a large, warm towel.

He surprised me when he led me back to the bed, then gently lowered me. I needed to get home, and I wasn't sure my body could go another round. We were insatiable together. Explosive even. I suspected we'd end up fucking each other to death if left unsupervised.

"Pierce," I said, exhaustion overtaking me. I still needed to call for an Uber and find my underwear. Not necessarily in that order.

"Shh," he said, climbing in the bed beside me.

What was he doing?

He pulled a fresh, new comforter over both of us. Then I felt him unbind my hands. I was about to take my blindfold off when I felt his hands gently lift the silk from my eyes for me. I blinked a couple of times. I'm sure they were a mess between my makeup, the heat, and all our passion. But I was too tired to care.

"Pierce," I said again. I didn't want to, but I knew I should leave. "I need to call for a ride home before it gets any later."

"You're not getting a cab," he said, his eyes tenderly taking in my face. He leaned in and slowly slid his tongue over my lips. "It's nearly five in the morning, and you're in a straight-up sex haze. There's no way I'm sending you home—not in a cab, or otherwise," he said, tucking a strand of my long, dark hair behind my ear. "Let's sleep it off, then we'll go from there, okay? You need some rest."

I couldn't disagree. "You're sure?" I asked quietly, already on my way to dreamland.

The last thing I remembered was a soft kiss on my forehead as I drifted off. I could've sworn I heard "Sweet dreams, birthday girl."

CHAPTER EIGHT

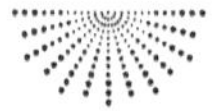

I HAD NO CLUE what time it was when I woke up, but sunlight was streaming in through the windows and Pierce wasn't next to me. I glanced around the room, unsure of what to do. Put my costume back on and then do the walk of shame? It was one thing to open yourself up to a stranger like that hidden behind the veil of night, but it was broad daylight now, and I suddenly found myself regretting staying over. I made my way to the bathroom to assess the damage. Eyeliner was in places it shouldn't be. I'd fallen asleep with whatever makeup was still on last night. Erm—early this morning, actually.

I hopped in the shower and ran the water hot, scalding all the sinful memories from my body. Sure, the man was a fucking demi-god. But I didn't know him any better than a random man off the street. I'd let him take me in ways no one ever had before and use my body as his personal playground. And now I had to face him, in my Maleficent costume no less. I groaned, closing my eyes as I dropped my head under the powerful sprays of water hitting my head and my body.

It was like getting an all-over massage, and I desperately needed it after last night.

I heard the shower door open but didn't have the guts to look up into those piercing blue eyes in the bright light of day. He stepped in, pulling me flush against his body. I sank gratefully against his chest as he wrapped his arms around me. Oddly enough, now that he was here, I felt more at ease.

"You're finally awake."

"What time is it?" I groaned.

"Two," he answered. "Hope you didn't have anywhere to be?"

Crap! I'd forgotten to call Lindy. She was probably a wreck by now, worried about me. "No," I said. "But my best friend is going to kill me."

"Don't worry. I've already had a nice, long talk with her."

I whipped my head up to look at him. "What?"

"Your phone was ringing off the hook all morning, so I assumed it was pretty important. I saw it was from your 'bestie,' since you have her programmed that way. So, I answered," he said, shrugging. "Figured she was pretty worried."

"Oh. Um, thank you?"

"Lindy is quite nice, by the way," Pierce said with a chuckle. "After she calmed down and I assured her you were safe, that is. She made me send a picture of you sleeping peacefully."

I groaned. "You didn't."

"You're really cute when you sleep."

"I passed out hard," I admitted, laughing. I leaned back and dipped my head under the spray so I could finish washing and get out. I was starving.

But I felt Pierce growing hard against my stomach, and I quickly forgot about food. I inhaled sharply when his mouth closed around my nipple, clearly on the same page as me. His tongue was every bit as hot and skilled as I remembered. Memories of our sordid night together ripped through me, turning me on all over again.

My hands went to his head, my back arching toward him. My damn body was on autopilot around him, and I couldn't stop my libido from overreacting if I tried. But, really . . . I had no interest in trying to make it stop. Pierce sparked something so deep and primal in me every time I was around him. His mouth was both my filthiest sin and most reverent hallelujah.

What was the harm in one more go?

~

THERE WAS NO such thing as "one more go" with Pierce. He was a fucking machine. Literally. I'm not sure one surface of his hotel room went untouched by my ass. Pierce loaned me a pair of sweatpants that I had to cinch at the waist, they were so big on me, and a college sweatshirt—Princeton no less. Then he asked me to stay for dinner before heading home. How could I say no?

He called his driver to pull around and wait for me at the front entrance, but before I left his room, he pulled me in for one last hug.

"I had an amazing weekend with you, Brynn," he said.

Ugh. This was going to be awkward, I could just feel it. Instead of having a meet-cute, we were about to have a dump-disaster. I was officially coining the term.

I didn't need reassurances or fake intentions. It was what it was—really amazing, earth-shattering sex. Okay, okay. So, maybe the best sex of my life. But still.

That's all this was.

"Me too," I said. "Thanks for making it a birthday I'll never forget."

"And how old are you now, Miss Hartley?"

"Twenty-eight," I said, glancing at his face for a reaction. I knew he was older than I was. I'd seen his driver's license. But age was just a number, and he wasn't *that* much older than me. What was a mere eleven years between friends, right?

He groaned.

"Is that a problem, Mr. Abrams? Because I'm kind of thinking you should've asked a little earlier if it was."

"Not at all," he said, tucking a hair behind my ear. "Everything about you just makes my dick twitch." He shrugged sheepishly.

I couldn't help but grin with satisfaction and give myself a mental high-five.

"Good," I said. "It doesn't matter anyway, right? You live in New York, and I live in Charlotte. This was never going to be anything more than a one-night stand."

Pierce surprised me by pulling me in for a deeply passionate last kiss, devouring my mouth, and leaving me in a near puddle of my hormones again. When he pulled back, I was breathing heavy and trying to regain my focus so I could leave in one piece.

"I'm here on business all week, Brynn," he murmured quietly. Suggestively. "And I'll be coming to Charlotte every week for the foreseeable future."

Oh. Well . . . crap. That just complicated things.

He gripped the back of my hair and forced me to look up at him. My nipples instantly hardened. "There's a lot we could still explore together—that is, if Brynn Hartley is single."

"Again, I'm kind of thinking you maybe should've asked me that a little earlier, Mr. Abrams," I said, deflecting.

I mean, was the man serious?

He growled. "Tell me you don't have a fucking boyfriend, Brynn."

"I don't, geez. I'm not that kind of girl," I said. Then I burst out laughing.

"What's so funny?" he asked, his eyes stormy.

"I just had a one-night stand with a complete stranger, that pretty much rivals any sex I've ever had—and I'm worried about not being perceived as 'that kind of girl'?" I snickered. "It's kind of too late for that, isn't it?"

"I don't see you as anything like that. We're two healthy, consenting adults with compatible sex drives and kinks. There's nothing wrong with exploring that together. Even if it was just one night. But I'd rather convince you to see me again."

"You mean fuck you again?" I asked bluntly.

He gripped my ass possessively and pulled my body flush against his. "That, too, baby girl. But it doesn't have to be *only* that. I'm a pure delight once you get to know me. That is," he said, holding me captive with his baby blues, "if you can keep your hands off me long enough to try."

I couldn't help but grin. It was tempting.

"Look, I haven't slept much over the last few days. I probably need a little space before making any decisions because it's too hard to think when you're all up in my personal space with your sexy masculinity and shit."

"You have such a way with words."

"You have no idea," I said, laughing.

He leaned in so close I could feel his breath on my neck. "Let's make a deal. Take tonight to get some sleep—because you're going to need it if you agree to see me again this week."

My insides actually *purred* at the thought of letting him control my body again that way.

"I put my number in your phone, along with a little picture. I want you to think about me all day tomorrow when you're at work. Remember how I owned your pussy, Brynn. And your ass," he said, squeezing it with his other hand.

I bit my lip. I needed to calm my fucking reaction around him.

He pulled something from his pocket and handed it to me, closing my fingers around it as he had with the key card on Friday. "When you're at work tomorrow, think about me and all the ways I can make your body come, beautiful angel."

Only this time, I didn't wait to see what he'd given me. I looked down at the black vice-like binder clip and gasped. *Well, shit.*

"I want you thinking of me all fucking day, Brynn. Every time you see one of these, I want you to remember how I made you come just by playing with your nipples," he whispered, making me wet all over again. "Then meet me at Havana's after work for some drinks if you're willing to give me more than just one night."

It was tempting. So tempting.

A harmless little affair—just sex. No strings attached.

With a man who rocked my fucking world this weekend.

I knew there was no way I wouldn't be waiting at Havana's tomorrow night, dripping wet and ready for him. Nothing could stop me from having Pierce in my arms one more time.

CHAPTER NINE

"YOU ARE CERTIFIABLY my hero," Lindy said, giggling with me in the office the next morning. It was easy to forget about my crappy job situation when I was recalling my sex-filled weekend with my bestie. "And here I thought Walter and I were adventurous."

"Lindy, you call the man Daddy. I'm pretty sure there's a lot you're not telling me."

She shrugged. "Well, we do have a nondisclosure agreement."

Wait. What?

Before I could ask her if she was serious, Dan knocked on my partially opened door. "Morning, ladies," he said, handing us both our favorite caffeinated beverages of choice. Lindy liked her chai tea lattes, while I preferred coffee, chocolate, and caramel—in that order.

I took a sip of my hot mocha, licking my lips and relishing the sugary high. "Dan, you are going to make some woman so happy someday."

"Could be someday soon, if she'd give me a chance." He winked at Lindy.

"You're incorrigible," she said.

"Have you all met the new boss yet?" Dan asked casually.

I nearly spit out my drink. "What? What do you mean?"

"You haven't heard?" he asked, trying to sound nonchalant. He shut the door and sat down beside Lindy. "Carlisa went into early labor this weekend!"

"She what?" Lindy squeaked. She glanced nervously at me and knew I was about to blow a fuse. "Does that mean her replacement is here? And we're not even getting the warm and fuzzy handoff we were promised?"

Dan shook his head. "She sent an email late last night—from the hospital. She was intending to introduce her replacement today, until this happened. Guess he's getting his feet wet a little quicker than he intended."

"So it's a 'he,' then?" I asked, scoffing. Of course it was. God forbid Carlisa hire a qualified woman internally.

"Yep," Dan said. "And"—he glanced down at his watch—"we're meeting him in ten minutes, in conference room B. Don't be late."

He stood and toasted his coffee mug in the air on his way out.

I glanced at Lindy and groaned, putting my head in my hands. Well, at least Pierce had been a healthy distraction this weekend. I'd nearly forgotten about having to face Carlisa's replacement today—my new archnemesis.

I would need to exorcise my demons on the poor man later. The idea of being with Pierce again like that brought a smile to my lips, despite what I was about to face.

"Oh my god!" Lindy hissed. "You're thinking about *that man* again, aren't you?"

"*That man* has a name," I reminded her. "And you were quite friendly with him yesterday, I heard."

"Well, you did forget to call me to let me know you were safe," she said, pouting.

"True, but that was only because he had me kinda tied up all weekend," I said.

She burst out laughing. "Come on, Brynn. Let's go face this monster. If we have to put up with an outsider for the next six weeks, let's give him hell."

WE ALL SAT around the conference room, quieter than normal. Even Shay wasn't being her usually vocal, bitchy self.

"Has anyone met him yet?" I asked, looking around at all the lead editors.

Everyone shook their heads no.

Hmm. Well then.

I took a deep breath. I mean, there was nothing I could do about the situation. Carlisa had already hired the man to take her place for the next six weeks. I'd have to grin and bear it if I wanted to stay in his good graces and have any chance of future advancement here. It sucked, but it was my current reality.

Just then the conference room door opened, and I raised my eyes with everyone else to see who was walking in.

Black, expensively tailored suit. Dark brown, almost black hair. Piercing blue eyes. Lion cufflinks.

No! I screamed inside. *No, no, no, no, no!*

Why was Pierce Abrams in *my* conference room?

I shot a panicked look at Lindy, and she shared one right back. Pierce hadn't seen me yet, and I was seriously tempted to slide under the table and hide. When he got to the head of the room, he set his things on the conference room table.

I glanced at my lap quickly, hoping he wouldn't recognize me. That's when I felt the heat and the weight of his gaze bearing down on me. The cells of my body didn't need to make eye contact to recognize that all-consuming intensity Pierce had scorched on my body with all weekend.

By the time I had the nerve to glance back up, his eyes had moved onto someone else, never missing a beat.

"Good morning, everyone," he said, starting the meeting. I honestly can't remember a thing he said after that because I think I had an out-of-body experience to preserve my sanity.

I'd let my new boss take my backside virginity, for god's sake. He'd buried his face between my thighs, and I'd let him clamp binder clips over my nipples, bringing me both the sharp sting of pain and euphoric pleasure all at once. *And I loved it all.*

I was certain I was about to have a panic attack.

Luckily, before I knew what was happening, everyone started getting up to leave. The meeting was over. I just sat there, feeling numb inside. *How* could I face this man with any modicum of self-respect? I wanted the earth to open and swallow me whole.

Kind of like what you did to him this weekend? the little devil on my shoulder whispered.

I jumped up from my seat and bolted from the room, not even waiting for Lindy. I closed my office door and dropped my head to my desk. What the actual fuck was I going to do?

The door opened, and Lindy's cute little swish of blond hair caught my eye as she peeked her head in. "Can I come in?" she asked. She *never* asked. This was bad.

As soon as she closed the door, I stage whispered, "What the fuck am I supposed to do with this?"

She was trying her hardest not to laugh.

"Are you serious right now?" I asked. "This is *not* in the least bit funny! This is my career."

"Maybe you'll get a promotion after all," she snickered.

"Lindy!"

"Sorry, sorry," she said, but she didn't look sorry. Not even the tiniest bit. "It's not as bad as you think, Brynn."

"Lindy," I hissed between clenched teeth, "I let the man throat-fuck me upside down."

Her eyes grew wide with that bit of information.

"Not so funny now, is it?"

"I'm sorry," she said truthfully. "But I really don't think it's quite as bad as you think."

"It's exactly as bad as I think!"

Just then my intercom light blinked, so I answered the call from our PA. "Yes, Rhonda?"

"Mr. Abrams is setting up one-on-one meetings with all the editorial heads and is requesting a five o'clock for yours. Can I confirm?"

Five? Why at five? To make me sit here and panic all day? To give me more time to go out of my fucking mind waiting? Was this a power play?

Ugh!

"That's fine, Rhonda. Thank you."

"Before you hang up, can you tell Lindy that hers is at four?"

"Thanks, Rhonda!" Lindy called out.

I hung up the phone and chewed my lower lip. "How am I supposed to sit here and not obsess about this all day?" I moaned. "I'm not going to get an ounce of work done, and I have a huge deadline for the Megan Morris romance I'm working on."

"Is that the throbbing one?" she asked, smirking.

"Stop talking about throbbing!" I practically yelled.

Lindy burst out laughing. "Oh, girl. You've got it bad."

I stood and walked around the desk. "You have no idea," I told her, lifting the hem of my skirt and turning slightly, showing her my backside. I was wearing the sexiest little bra and panty set under my outfit today, in anticipation of seeing *Pierce* again later. She was getting a nice, full shot of my ass because the thong I'd chosen didn't cover much.

"Whoa," she said, leaning in and looking closer.

There was a trail of small bruises along my thighs and backside. I'd seen them in the mirror this morning when I got dressed. What can I say? He'd literally hammered me to orgasm multiple times. There'd been no gentleness as we ravaged each other's bodies this weekend. My body ached in the most sinfully, sexually used-and-abused kind of way. It would've been thrilling, had the same man not walked into *my* conference room introducing himself as *my* new boss. Not only that, but to make matters worse, he was also the thief who took *my* promotion from me!

"Yeah, things got a little heated."

"Definitely my hero," she said in awe. Her phone buzzed and she glanced down, then squealed. "Well, if this isn't perfect timing!"

She flashed her phone in front of me for a millisecond before opening our daily horoscopes. She read them and raised her eyebrows. "Hmm" was all she said, not giving anything away.

"Well?" I demanded at her not-so-subtle, cryptic *hmm*.

"Just the possibility of a marriage proposal," she said, shimmying her shoulders like Shaquille O'Neal.

"That better be for you," I snarled.

She laughed. "Most definitely. Want me to read yours or send it to you?"

I sighed. "Send it to me, please. I need to get back to my edits anyway."

"Sent," she said, heading for the door. "Want any company for lunch today?"

"Can't. I have to power through this. It's my most important edit left this year."

"Okay. Good luck!" she said. Then she paused at the door before turning back to me. "Brynn, don't get in your head over this. I know how deep and emotional you can get sometimes. Wait to see what he has to say later. You never know. He could surprise you."

I harrumphed, feeling salty about the whole thing.

"Read the horoscope too. I mean it," she said before disappearing. I opened the link from Lindy's text, picked up my now-cold coffee, and read.

SCORPIO
Your Daily Horoscope for
Monday, November 1

> Feeling the burn yet, Scorpio? As with most things you take on, this fiery new passion you're fueling is shrouded in sexual intensity, charm, and a dash of mystery. Don't forget to lean on your intuition and intelligence. Not everything is as straightforward as it seems—but your protective nature will soon help you determine where your loyalty lies.
>
> While your career may feel at a stalemate, things are just heating up! Get ready to get creative, and be sure to use your cleverness, wisdom, and natural magnetism to maneuver the sticky situation you're now in.

> But don't forget! What goes around comes back around. Ask yourself—is it better to be consumed by the flame or keep your heart protected? Which path will you choose when push comes to shove and a second chance at love comes knocking at your door?
>
> As with all matters, the answers are already written in the stars.

I buzzed Lindy right away. "What is this bullshit? Mystery, things coming back around, loyalty? I can't with all this cloak-and-dagger crap! Why doesn't someone just write a horoscope that says something like 'Today you'll win a million bucks. The guy at the coffee shop has a crush on you. Oh, and don't take the L today.' Now, shit like that, I would pay for!"

"That's called a psychic, Brynn. Two totally different things. Want me to take you to mine?"

Even though she could see me, I shook my head. I had enough of a mess on my hands without someone else confusing things even more.

"No," I said with a sigh. "But I'm done with my horoscope. I can't make heads or tails of it today."

"Guess what I found out, though," Lindy piped in, ever the optimist to my broody nature.

"Lay it on me," I said, rolling my eyes as I picked up the manuscript I was working on.

I was only half listening when I heard Lindy say, "He's a Leo, you know."

"Who's a Leo?" I asked. My computer notification went off, so I clicked open my email inbox and scrolled as Lindy started reading again.

"Well, according to LiveAbout, they say that Leos and Scorpios are *legendary* lovers," she said. "And I quote: 'Where passion meets fierce loyalty and spikes in fiery conflict. Leo in love is proud, generous, and demanding. Scorpio in love is power-wise and enveloping . . . The Leo and Scorpio alliance is about stirring the creative cauldron, for self-expression and manifesting all they desire.' End quote," she said, clearly proud of her discovery.

"Sorry, Linds. Who's a Leo?"

"Oh my god, were you not even listening? Pierce Abrams—that's who!"

"Aren't Leos fire signs, though?"

"Yes! But they're also romantic and creative. They're the heroes," she said dramatically.

"Do I need a hero? Because I'm fairly sure I don't."

"Okay, fine. So *I* enjoy the hero. But they're also ambitious, loyal, generous—"

"Egotistical, stubborn, domineering," I reminded her.

"Domineering can be good," she said. "I didn't hear you complaining after this weekend."

"Touché," I said, laughing. "But it doesn't matter anyway, Linds. He's my *boss.*"

"Boss-schmoss," she said dismissively. "He's fucking gorgeous, Brynn."

I groaned. She didn't need to tell me that. I remembered every inch of his chiseled form. He was bigger than men I'd dated in the past—muscle-wise, obviously. Well, and *that,* too, if I was being honest. His back was sculpted in a gym, with muscles I didn't know existed. And his biceps. Dear god, he was able to pick me up and fling me around like I weighed next to nothing. Okay. So maybe a *little* domineering wasn't so bad.

"I need to stop thinking about how gorgeous he is and figure out how I'm going to get out of this mess!" I hissed.

My computer dinged again. It was another incoming message from an agency whose name I didn't recognize.

"Look, I gotta go," I said. "My emails are backing up, and I've reread this same paragraph about ten times now."

"Fine. *Work*, then," she said, as if that wasn't what we were actually being paid to do. I forgot sometimes that her work ethic and personal ambition weren't quite as driven as mine.

I clicked open the email and started reading, confused. I skipped down to the end of the message and gasped when I saw the signature line.

Noah Chance.

Shivers raced up my arms as if I'd seen a ghost. And I practically had.

Why was my best friend from childhood—the boy I'd once promised to marry—contacting me after nearly eighteen years of silence?

Only one way to find out.

CHAPTER TEN

I READ THE EMAIL again for a third time. My hands shook as I scrolled down the screen and nearly memorized each word.

Dear Brynn,

Hello, old friend. It's been a while. Sorry to contact you this way, after so many years of silence. But when I saw that you, too, were in the publishing field, and at the exact firm I needed to get in touch with—well, it felt like fate, to say the least.

Business first, then pleasure.

Our agency, Chance and Chambers Creative, is looking for representation for one of our best-selling authors. You may have heard of her. She has a series of well-known young adult dystopian romance novels that have been optioned for film rights. She is currently writing a modern-day series based on the zodiac signs—charming, right? While her dystopian novels are a sure-fire sell, publishers in the UK are skeptical about the crossover and backing her new contemporary romance series.

I, however, believe in Eve Donohue, with every fiber of my being. Based on her initial proposal, I know this series has massive reach and sales potential. I'm taking a chance and am reaching out to you because I've seen Sterling and Masters's track record, and I'm confident Eve Donohue would be an asset to your portfolio.

I'd like to share not only her full twelve-book Written in the Stars series proposal with you but also the completed first book in the collection—Diamond in the Rough, a rags-to-riches story about an Aries celebrity who rises to fame too quickly. It's a second-chance romance—and who doesn't love those?

I know Carlisa Mayhew is the editorial executive at Sterling and Masters, but I have it on good authority that she is heading on maternity leave soon. It was a stroke of good luck that the contemporary romance editor is none other than my long-lost fiancée from childhood. 😉

I would love to hear from you on both a professional and personal level. Which brings me to the pleasure part of my correspondence.

I will be in Charlotte the week of 8 November. You may remember my grandmother, Loula Belle Darling, from when we were kids. When we moved to the UK, my parents never settled her estate back in Charlotte. However, they left me with quite the mess a few years ago when they both died.

If you recall, the property is a historic home in Dilworth. I'm headed to Charlotte to handle the estate sale and get her house on the market. It breaks my heart to part with a family home, but it doesn't make sense for me to hold on to it with me being in London.

I know it has been a good many years since we've seen one another, Brynn. And I know we were just children when we were friends. But I have held the memory of you with me all these years. I still remember frogging with you in the summers, water skiing at my parents' lake house, and slaying dragons together. Even then, you were a fierce, independent badass who would go to the ends of the earth to protect your friends. It was something I always loved about you. You were also the best tree climber I'd ever laid eyes on. Those are important things to a twelve-year-old boy.

Well, that, and the fact that you were my first kiss.

A guy can't just forget something like that, pigtails.

I hope you still hold our time together fondly in your heart and are open to seeing me again when I'm back in town.

I will have my personal assistant contact you this week to set up a time for us to meet professionally. Please feel free to invite whoever needs to be at that meeting with you to make a decision. We have four other agencies we are visiting whilst in the States, but I wanted to give Sterling and Masters first rights of refusal on this special series, given our history together.

Please find attached the entire proposal as well as a PDF file of book one for your reading pleasure. I think you'll find the lead character's story arc compelling and her relationships deeply romantic. Some might say fated even.

Perhaps like our own story. Wouldn't that be something after all these years and all these miles between us? I look forward to finding out soon, Brynn Hartley.

Cheers!

Yours sincerely,
Noah Chance

I picked up my phone and texted Lindy to come back to my office ASAP. Two minutes later, the door opened, and Lindy flopped down into one of my guest chairs.

"Just can't live without me, can you?"

"Of course I can't, sweet cheeks," I said, grinning at her. She looked adorable today with her new shorter hairstyle pin straight. She was wearing a black, open-collared V-neck jumper that looked like a man's business suit but with flared pant legs and short, flared white sleeves. Her heels were nude, and she had on large silver hoops.

"You look cute today, by the way," I said. I felt bad that my own drama had overtaken any focus on Lindy this morning. "How did Walter like your, um, red leather surprise Saturday night?"

"I was wondering how long it was going to take you to ask that," she teased. "Let's just say it was a huge hit. And, it might've had a matching collar and leash that I added back to the ensemble when we got home."

"Lindy!" I said, genuinely shocked.

"What?" She shrugged. "Can't a girl like to be walked by her daddy?"

"On a leash, though?" I gaped at her.

"Don't knock it till you try it," she said, winking.

I suddenly had a vision of myself in a black leather Peter Pan collar with a golden chain attached. In my fantasy, I was crawling along the conference room table, Pierce holding the other end of the lead.

I swallowed, suddenly seeing the appeal.

"Okay, then," I said and made a mental note. "But back to why I texted. You are *never* going to believe who I heard from today."

I proceeded to fill her in on everything, then showed her the email so she could read it word for word. "Well?" I asked, gnawing at the skin near my thumbnail.

"Well what? I assume you're going to catch up with him, right?"

"I don't know. I mean—should I?"

"Are you taking the business meeting?"

I thought about it for about point two seconds. "Of course I am. Hello! It's Eve fucking Donohue! Even I know who that is. It would be foolish not to read her manuscript."

"So that has nothing to do with the handsome literary agent presenting it, then? It's just strictly professional?"

"Who said he was handsome?"

Lindy shrugged. "I just assumed if you kissed him, he was probably at least cute when he was a kid."

I nodded, remembering the adorable towheaded boy next door. "I haven't seen him in eighteen years, Lindy. That's a long time to change."

"Have you looked him up?"

"No!" I said, exasperated. "I literally texted you the minute I was done reading his email!"

"Okay, okay . . . no need to get huffy. Let's find him, shall we?"

"Why have I never thought to do this before?" I asked.

"Because you never enlisted my help," she said. "Well, hello, Noah Chance," she said, biting the corner of her mouth.

"For fuck's sake, he can't be that cute," I insisted.

She sent me a link, which I immediately opened. I swallowed hard. "Well, hello, Noah Chance," I said. "I'll be damned."

The cute twelve-year-old kid I'd kissed was no longer the skinny, freckle-faced boy I remembered. He'd somehow morphed into the love child of David Beckham, Logan Macrae, and Jack Butland. And holy hell . . . all I could think of now was a foursome with those three delicious men. What in the world had gotten into me?

"If you don't meet with him, I will," Lindy offered.

"You're not even in the romance department," I reminded her.

"I meant for the personal portion of his letter," she teased.

"Lindy! You're practically married," I pointed out.

She waved her hand. "Then he better put a ring on it."

I laughed. "Don't let Dan hear you say that. He'd be devastated if you ditched Walter and didn't immediately call him up."

"What can I say?" she said, shrugging. "I'm into blonds."

My mouth hung open. "Walter's blond?"

"Oh, shut up!" she said with a laugh. "He's not *that* old."

"I'm just kidding," I teased. Kind of. "So, seriously. What do I say? I mean, I'm in a little bit of a pickle here already with Pierce. Can you just imagine if I bring *him* into a meeting with my childhood crush? Talk about awkward overload!"

"Well, neither really *has* to know, right?"

I considered that for a moment. I wasn't dating either of the guys, I just had history with them both. And it seemed as if they'd both be in my future to some degree now. That is, if the book deal went through. This could get complicated quickly.

One step at a time.

I took a deep breath. "I don't even know if I'll have a job after today, Brynn. I mean, Pierce could fire me."

"No, he can't," she insisted. "You could sue Sterling and Masters if he did. Neither of you knew he was going to be your boss. He can't hold that against you."

"How in the world am I going to do this, though?" I asked her earnestly. "This weekend with Pierce was . . . mind-blowing. To say the least. You know I'm not shy about sex, Lindy. I mean, hello! I love everything about it. But Pierce. He is next level. There's just something so magnetic about him. It was like I was being drawn to him and was completely helpless to any other outcome. From the first time he kissed me, I knew I was a goner. I mean, I seriously could have fucked him right there in Founders Hall. Does that make any sense?"

"Yeah," she said, sighing. "That's how I feel about Walter. I know he doesn't make sense to everyone, and he might not look like Pierce, but that's exactly how I *feel* about him. It's like he has my pussy on this invisible string, and all he does is flick it and I'm at his feet asking him what position he wants me in."

I laughed. Now *that* was an image I'd never be able to unsee.

"I get it," I said. And I really did after this weekend. "I let that man do things to my body I never even let Nick do, Lindy. It's not that I didn't love Nick, or that we didn't have amazing sex. Well, I guess toward the end it wasn't so amazing. But you know what I mean."

"I know exactly what you mean. You wouldn't believe the things I let Walter do to me. It reminds me of a quote from a book I read once by Nora Roberts. I know she's not everyone's cup of tea, but I personally adore her. I mean, she writes romance just as easily as she does blood and gore. What's not to love?"

"Lindy!" I practically yelled. "Get on with it."

"Oh, yeah. Sorry!" she said, laughing. "So, I can't remember the name of the book or the exact quote," she said, and I rolled my eyes. "Hear me out. The main character says something that stuck with me over the years. It was about how when a woman truly tumbles with a man in bed, giving herself over completely while doing things so sinful they make her tremble, she can't help but want more, 'even as she pants to do them again' in the light of day."

"That's *exactly* how I feel," I said quietly, thinking of the way Pierce touched me. Licked me. Bit me, for heaven sake.

Lindy laughed as she watched me. "Yeah, you've got it bad. You're panting to do them again, all right."

"I don't know exactly *what* it is about him, Linds. I mean, sure. He's hot as all get-out. But my god. I think we fucked about seven times in less than twenty-four hours. And," I whispered, looking around even though we were completely alone, "I had anal for the first time."

"Shut your face!" Lindy said, squealing. "And?"

"And what?"

"Did you love it?"

I nodded. "I kind of did. I mean, I never *thought* I'd like that. But my god. The man just knows how to make everything come alive, you know? I mean, I had orgasms that had orgasms."

"What are we even talking about again?" Lindy asked dreamily.

"Fuck if I know," I said. "But I need to go take a walk or something because I'm all kinds of frustrated now."

"Girl, you need to keep a vibrator in your desk. That's what I do."

"What?" I gawked at my best friend like she had two heads.

"Well, sometimes a girl has needs and her Walter's not around. So, I pull up some porn on my phone, pop in my clit-sucking vibrator, and let Tracy's Dog go to town."

"I do not even want to know what you're talking about," I said.

"I swear I'm getting you one for your birthday," she said, standing up. "Oh, wait. That was Saturday. Fuck."

"I don't need a birthday gift, Lindy. You're all I need. Thanks for talking this out with me."

"Anytime. Now, I'll be on Do Not Disturb for the next half hour, so don't text me. All this sex talk got me fired up."

I closed my eyes. "I really wish I didn't know all this about you."

"Don't be jealous, bitch," she said, flouncing from my office.

I sighed. She was right. I *was* frustrated. That was the problem.

Ever since yesterday, all I could think about was meeting up with Pierce tonight. And now? The only meeting I'd be doing with him was in a conference room. And not in the fun way I'd imagined while talking with Lindy.

I could *not* go in there all sexually charged up like this. I'd be a fucking live wire and embarrass myself. I used the intercom to call Rhonda. "I need to run to the drug store over my lunch break. Forward all my calls for the rest of the afternoon. When I get back, I need to be uninterrupted to finish these edits today. Keep everyone out—including Lindy."

"Will do, Miss Hartley," she said pleasantly.

By the time I got back from grabbing my lunch and going to the drugstore, it was one o'clock. I had four hours until I needed to face Mr. Abrams. My insides ached just thinking about seeing him again.

I pulled out my phone and did a search on Pierce Abrams. It didn't take long for me to find dozens of images of him in the news. I ignored the stories and went straight for the pics. I found one of him in a tux, his dark brown hair slicked back at a red-carpet event. He had a beard in this picture, and it was all kinds of hot and distracting.

I was about to turn on the "personal massager" that I bought from CVS when I thought better of it. If I was going to go into a meeting with Pierce, I needed to *not* think about him that way right before I walked in. So, instead, I pulled up some pictures of my childhood best friend again. There were dozens of them because he'd played football in university. I enlarged one of the images of Noah on the field, shirtless, after he scored. His hair was a rich, sun-kissed golden blond, bordering on light brown. He had a severe case of five o'clock shadow going on, his beard almost looking a little ginger in the light. And his sexy hazel eyes were lasered back at me, his arms flexing in victory.

He was hot, sweaty, and manly.

Yeah, that did it for me. I closed my eyes and cataloged that image into my brain, willing myself not to let my mind wander back to Pierce. Instead I rehashed Noah's words in my head as I raised my skirt and pressed the bulbous massager head over my clit.

"Perhaps like our own story."

Would we have an *us* story? Or would his return home be nothing more than a simple reunion between old friends?

I tried to imagine what it would be like to kiss Noah again, this time as the sexy thirty-year-old man I'd seen online. The scratch of his beard, the golden skin beneath my fingertips. Would it feel like coming home? Would I get butterflies again?

But as much as I tried, it wasn't Noah's face that kept coming to the front of my mind as I melted under the steady thrum of my personal massager.

I was officially screwed, and not in a good way either.

CHAPTER ELEVEN

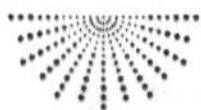

HE ACTUALLY MADE me wait. I already felt like I was going to throw up and couldn't concentrate on Megan Morris's book to save my life. The mini "massage" session earlier did nothing more than stoke the slow-burning embers already left by Pierce yesterday. It didn't help that Lindy never popped by my office after her meeting with our new boss, and she wasn't answering my calls either.

To pass the time, I followed up with Noah's PA and set an appointment for the following Tuesday morning to discuss Eve Donohue's book—which meant this week would be nonstop busy as I finished the project I was currently working on *and* worked my way through hers. But if I could land Eve Donohue for Sterling and Masters, it would be a real coup. Something Carlisa wouldn't be able to overlook when she got back. I also carved out time to respond to Noah on a personal level because, if I was being truthful with myself, his email touched me in a surprising, tender way.

I used to dream about Noah when I was a teenager, imagining where he lived, who he went to school with, and what he'd grown up to look like. Over the years, I had to let my childhood fantasy slip away and embrace the messy, passionate, complex life that was right in front of me. That didn't mean, though, that the romantic in me didn't sometimes fantasize about Noah showing up one day. My heart hammered at the idea that "someday" was here, and that in a week, we'd be face to face again. The thought made my stomach do somersaults. I couldn't wait to tell Grampa. Surely, he'd remember Noah.

At least, I hoped he would.

Just when I was about to throw in the towel, Rhonda buzzed my intercom and told me that Pierce would see me now. It was seven freaking thirty. I took a deep breath and steeled myself, making my way into the common area. That's when I realized I had no idea where Pierce's office was. I found Rhonda packing up her things to go home.

"Sorry, Rhonda, but can you tell me which office Pierce is using? I realized it wasn't on the original invite, and I haven't received an updated one from him."

"Of course, dear. He's in the large corner office, right next to yours. The CIO's old office."

I swallowed. He'd been right next door to me all day long?

My lips went dry, and I felt light-headed.

"Are you okay?" Rhonda asked. "Can I get you a water or something?"

"No, I'm fine," I said, feeling foolish. "Just surprised, I guess, that he took an office bigger than Carlisa's."

"Well, he couldn't have hers, since she's coming back," she pointed out.

Don't remind me.

"Right. Well, have a nice evening, Rhonda!" I said, making my way back toward my office. This made it even stranger that Lindy hadn't stopped by after her meeting. She could've at least texted me to give me a heads-up. This would've been a "nice to know."

Pierce's door was closed. His office had glass windows, like all the formal office spaces on our floor. Junior associates sat in the common area in cubicles, but department leads got closed-door offices. It was a perk I was quite happy about. I'd spent too many years in "the pit," as we jokingly called it.

I knocked on Pierce's door and bit my lower lip. I thought he would call me in and make me sit across from him at his desk, so my stomach was all twisted in knots. Instead, he surprised me when he opened the door, grinned, and pulled me inside—and straight into his arms.

I wasn't prepared for the heat of his lips as his mouth crashed against mine. Or the way his hands possessively pulled me close to his body, wrapping tightly up my back as if he couldn't get me close enough. I couldn't help the pull or the desire to kiss him back. I didn't think with my managing editor brain. I let emotions take over and did nothing but feel with my heart.

I felt *everything* that was in that kiss.

And I gave back just as much. All the emotions from our shotgun weekend bubbled forward, and I found myself hungry for Pierce in a way I'd never craved a man before.

It bordered on obsession.

When the kiss finally tempered and our energy subdued enough to breathe again, Pierce pulled back, looking down into my heart with his striking blue eyes.

"Well, this was a plot twist I didn't see coming," he said, his voice thick with emotion. He brushed my hair aside and ran his fingers along my neck, making my body shiver under his touch.

"I've been worried about seeing you all day," I admitted. "This isn't good, Pierce."

He laughed, pulling me further into his office. "No. It's great, actually."

I looked around his new office space. Somehow, he'd already had it decorated to his liking, giving the large space a complete facelift. I felt like I was getting a glimpse into the man.

The walls were now painted a soft, muted gunmetal gray, and floor-to-ceiling, open-backed bookcases lined the wall adjoining my office. A ginormous vintage art piece depicting an old record player hung on the wall between the bookcases, directly behind Pierce's desk, showcasing the creative side of his personality.

He'd had a bluish gray area rug brought in that was faded and distressed-washed, and it covered nearly all the hardwood floor. And the man's desk was a work of art—all golden oak, metal, and modern. A funky Edison bulb chandelier gave him some ambient light over his desk and was just a cool statement piece.

"Impressive," I said. As I glanced over at the seating area with the pecan-colored Denmark sofa and two conversation chairs, something didn't add up. One thing was clear: Pierce was most definitely here to stay. He wouldn't have invested this kind of money into personalizing his office otherwise.

While the thought secretly thrilled me, my heart also sank a little as my dream of becoming the editorial executive deflated like a sad balloon. I had to come to terms with the fact that the man I'd slept with—but barely knew—was now my new boss.

"How are you doing?" he asked, studying me as I took in all the personal artifacts he'd lined his shelves with.

"About as good as I can be after finding out my torrid one-night stand is actually my new boss." I glanced at a framed picture of a men's ice hockey team. "Are you in here?"

"Princeton Tigers," he said proudly. "Lucky number twenty-eight," he said and winked. Now, what were the odds of that?

He pointed to one of the men in a large group of about thirty college guys posed out on the ice for their team portrait. His hair was a little shaggier then, and he had a lot more scruff. But his eyes were unmistakable and made him stand out in the crowd. Holy hell, he was hot as fuck in a hockey uniform. There was a second picture of him on the ice, body checking a player from an opposing team, his hockey stick in the air.

I was about to ask him where he wanted me to sit for our meeting, when I felt him come up behind me. He wrapped his arms around my waist as he had in the sauna, and he brushed my hair aside to pepper kisses along my throat. Goose bumps raced down my body, and it took everything inside me not to reach back and grab him. But I vowed to myself not to stroke my boss's cock within five minutes of our first one-on-one meeting.

"Pierce," I said, turning to face him. As much as I wanted to fall back into his arms again, we needed to have a serious conversation first.

"Have I ever told you how much I love hearing my name come out of that sexy little mouth of yours?"

"You mean in all of the four days we've known each other?" I asked, raising a brow.

He chuckled. "You're sharp. I like that."

"This isn't a game, Pierce. This is my career. One I've spent the last seven years building."

"I see," he said, nodding. "Okay, then let's talk." He waved me over toward the low-back leather sofa.

Thanks to Lindy, I now had the image in my mind of being on all fours, letting Pierce lead me to the sofa by a leash. I shook my head to clear the image, then sat down. He sat in one of the chairs opposite me, and I appreciated him giving me the breathing space.

"I know these are highly unusual circumstances we find ourselves in, Miss Hartley," he said, visibly trying not to smirk. "But I'm also starting to realize the benefits to our situation as well."

He reached for a file folder that was sitting on the small natural wood table between the two conversation chairs. "I see you came to Sterling and Masters right out of college. Impressive," he said as he scanned my file. "Top one percent of your class. Double major."

"None of that has any value compared to the work I do every day, though. It's the portfolio and relationships I've built over the years that make me the proudest of my accomplishments. And it's my authors who make what I do so rewarding. College ended seven years ago. Every day since then, I've busted my ass to make a name for myself here—and to get ahead. I made it known early on in my career that I was interested in advancing as far as I could."

"Now you're upset?" he asked. "Because an outsider came in to fill Carlisa's role while she's on maternity leave?"

I hated how he saw right through my hurts and desires.

"Yes," I admitted. "No one, me included, understood why she would hire an outsider—no offense—when we have several more-than-qualified internal candidates who have been working hard for an opportunity like this."

There was no point lying to him. Within a day he'd get enough gossip to fill in the blanks if I left them there. I'd rather take control of my future and tell him exactly where I stood—even if it meant leaving Sterling and Masters or offending him.

But he didn't seem upset. He seemed thoughtful.

His eyes dropped back to my file. "Hmm. You have some pretty impressive clients, Brynn."

"I do my best to curate the best in the genre at any given time."

"You have a few names I'm not familiar with," he pointed out.

"I do," I said proudly. "They're the genre's future. The best clients are the diamonds in the rough," I said, borrowing a line from Eve Donohue's story.

"I couldn't agree more," he said, "which will bring some interesting changes over the coming weeks. But I'm not ready to talk about that yet. I need to get a lay of the land first, study the office dynamics. I've already gotten a pretty complete picture after today."

He didn't have the whole picture, though. Because he was only being shown what people wanted him to see. He didn't *know* them like I did. He couldn't read the underlying intentions behind their perfected words like I could. It was a natural gift of mine and something I prided myself on. It's also why I knew I'd make an amazing leader, if given the chance. My intuition combined with my years of knowledge from this industry made me the best at what I did. I wasn't shy to admit that—or to make it known that I wanted Carlisa's job someday.

"There's a lot more than meets the eye," I said cautiously. "But I'm sure you know that, coming from a corporate background as you do."

He raised an eyebrow at me. "So, you've done your research today, too, I see."

"Yeah, though I didn't have much time," I said.

I hated the way I'd been taken by surprise earlier. I hated not being in the know. For the most part, I had my finger on the pulse of almost everything that went on in this company. That is, until Pierce came along. Everything started not going my way on Friday—and it was all because of him.

I suddenly had a sinking feeling in the pit of my stomach. I swallowed any last pride I had left because I had to know. And I *would* know if he was lying.

"Did you know this whole time?" I asked quietly.

Had he hand-selected me from Havana's for a reason? Was it more than just an instant attraction and chance encounter?

"Did you know who I was? On Friday when you bumped into me at Havana's? Or on Saturday, when you took me back to your hotel room to fuck my brains out?" I was sickened by the idea. I hated the way my voice shook, but it wasn't going to stop me from being heard. "Did you look through my file before today, Pierce?"

I gripped the edge of the couch, furious with my own stupidity for not seeing this sooner.

Pierce was out of his seat and next to me before I understood what was happening. My body was nearly shaking I was so distraught at the idea of him using me like that. Or that the weekend hadn't meant what I thought it had.

I would burn this motherfucker to the ground and walk away right now if that was the case. There was no way I'd work for him if he'd betrayed my trust like that.

"Look at me, Brynn," he said.

I had to know. So I did.

I raised my darkened eyes and met his square-on. He didn't look away. He let me read him, staring long and hard into the openings of his soul.

"I had no idea you worked here when I saw you Friday night in Havana's," he said. "There are a lot of businesses in this office building, and people from all over Uptown come to that bar. I'd had a shitty meeting with Carlisa and the executive team, and I needed to blow off some steam. I was walking out with some of my legal team, as well as some investors I do business with here, when I looked up and saw the most beautiful angel I'd ever laid eyes on wearing the saddest frown," he said. "It didn't belong on you."

Oh.

"The only part of our meeting that wasn't authentic was my just so happening to be there when you turned to leave. You hadn't seen me yet, but I couldn't leave fate to chance," he said. "I asked the guys to wait for me, and I sought you out. I could tell the woman in your group was making you uncomfortable, but there was a deeper sadness there too. I just wanted to make you smile. Maybe get your number. But I swear to god, Brynn, I didn't know you worked for Sterling and Masters then, or even on Saturday night. The fact that the fates threw you right back to me only made me want you even more. You were like this bright beacon in a room full of boring, gray corporate droids." He chuckled.

"The lights were flashing. The songs were loud. But you, Brynn," he said, running his hand down my arm, "you stood there dancing with that guy—Dan—without a care in the world. The sadness I'd seen Friday was at least momentarily gone. And when you wear your light, there's no one else in the fucking room."

I swallowed, unable to move. I guess that was a solid no.

He took my hand into his, rubbing the back with his thumb. "I would've moved heaven and earth to get you to agree to just a date with me that night. But then I put my hands on you, and all bets were off. I know you felt it too," he said with a near growl.

I bit my lower lip and nodded. I had. He knew I had. It was why I went back to the hotel with him. As tempting as the offer had been on Friday, it was a brush-off come on. But Saturday, I *felt* Pierce's energy. I'd *seen* him. And I had to have more. I had to feel the explosion of us coming together. Because I'd known that was exactly what it was going to be.

"I didn't intend to take you back to my hotel and fuck you like that, Brynn. Yeah, I mean"—he brushed his hand through his hair—"I *wanted* to sleep with you. I was hoping that's where it was going. But I didn't know it was going to turn into a freaking obsession to worship your body every single possible way my mind could conjure."

I wet my lips. So, he'd felt that part of it too. The inexplicable pull. The surrender.

"I believe you," I said softly. "I had to ask, Pierce. You understand why."

He lifted my hand and placed it over his heart. "Brynn, I didn't mean for this situation to happen. But I can't say I'm sorry it did. I'll never say that."

I nodded. "I know. But I can't let this ruin my career here. This weekend was amazing—okay, beyond amazing. Earth-shattering, for me anyway."

"It was for me too," he said quietly.

I could tell he wanted to taste me again. I saw the desire in his eyes. Noticed the way he watched my lips. I glanced down, trying to frame what I needed to say, when my eyes landed on his lap. The bulge of his cock strained against his suit pants, and I could instantly remember the feel of him as he slid inside me.

"This doesn't have to change anything," he said.

Lindy was right. He already had me panting to do all kinds of filthy things with him again.

"Remember what I told you in the hotel room, when I told you I wanted as much of you as I could get while I was here?"

I couldn't, really. But then again, I'd been in a complete and utter sex haze, and I probably would've sworn away my firstborn.

"I asked you to give up control with me. That during our time together, you would do whatever I asked of you. Do you remember that?"

I swallowed. I thought he'd meant for that one night. In his hotel room. That was all this was supposed to be.

He ran a finger over my bottom lip.

"You're so fucking perfect, Brynn. I know we have a lot more to talk about, but it's time to do something for me, something I've wanted since the minute I walked into that conference room and saw you sitting there all prim and proper and fucking decimated. I don't want to be the cause of that look," he said, pressing his thumb into my mouth.

I knew I should stop him. Tell him nothing like this could happen again. But I was already wet, even as my tongue wrapped around his thick finger. I closed my eyes and moaned, wishing it was his cock instead.

He pulled his thumb from my mouth and stood, leaving me confused, wanting, and on the brink of running.

"Get on your knees, Brynn. Kneel for me," he said as he ran his hand over his thick shaft through his pants.

It was already dark outside, and the backdrop was like a sea of stars as white city lights twinkled around us on the other side of his office windows. When I looked into Pierce's eyes, I understood that his request was more than just an order. It was a question, on the precipice of everything that *could* be.

He wanted me on my knees. He was asking me to meet him there.

Could I?

I knew if I did, there was no going back.

I felt as if I was standing on the edge of a massive cliff, looking out into a void of black space below me. If I opened my arms and closed my eyes, I could fall . . . trusting that he'd catch me somehow, someway.

Or I could take a step back and be safer—on more steady ground.

The click of the lock on his office door was like the warm flick of his tongue over my clit. My body jumped, already a bundle of nerves thinking about what he might do if I just slid off the couch and onto my knees like he'd asked.

"If I have to ask you again, I will put you over my knees and spank that sweet little ass of yours."

Asking time was over.

"That won't be necessary, Mr. Abrams," I said coyly. I stood up, meeting his gaze dead-on. I could tell he was confident. He knew I would fall to my knees for him. And it was sexier than anything I'd ever encountered.

My pussy constricted as I kneeled on the carpet. I sat back on my heels, my posture straight and my nipples puckering in anticipation. The soft whir of a motor drew my attention, and the office dimmed. I knew he'd closed the blinds to the city, shrouding us in just the seductive, ambient glow of the Edison bulbs. He slowly undid his belt as he walked toward me, his eyes never leaving mine. Then he unzipped his dress pants, pulled out his thick cock, and stroked it with one hand, while he swung his looped belt in the other.

"Tomorrow, you are to wear a black harness bra and lace panties to work," he said, getting closer. My pussy was noticeably wet already, and if he reached down, he would feel me sopping through my thong—the one I'd worn for him, ironically.

"I want you in a set of black thigh-high stockings and a matching garter belt. With black stiletto heels. If you don't have those things, I'll have a set shipped to your home this evening. Are we clear?"

"Yes, sir," I said, my palms getting sweatier the closer he got.

"Do you have those items?"

"No, sir."

"Size?"

"My bra is a 32B, and my panties are a small," I said.

"Shoes?"

"An eight."

"Skirt?"

"A six."

"Blouse and suit jacket?"

"Same, sir. About a size six, unless it runs big. Then a four."

He was standing above me now, his cock bouncing on its own accord. I remembered the delicious dichotomy of velvety soft skin over his rock-hard shaft.

"Are you wet for me yet?"

I nodded.

"Finger yourself, then," he commanded.

"Here?"

"Now," he said, rubbing his hand along his shaft.

I reached under my skirt and slid my hand beneath my panties. I was already a hot, wet mess for Pierce Abrams. I closed my eyes, slowly sliding two fingers into my slippery opening.

My fingers brushed my clit with each pass, the ache taking over. Oh, how I wanted his teeth on me. I needed the sweet relief only pressure could bring. I shuddered.

"What are you imagining, Brynn?"

It was as if he knew.

"I was imagining your teeth slowly teasing my clit. I need a bigger release than I can give myself."

"I know exactly what you need, baby girl."

He took off his suit jacket and laid it on the back of one of his chairs. Then he slowly rolled up the sleeves on his white dress shirt. I swear, I almost came watching him. Business suit porn could be an entire romance trope of its own.

"But I have a surprise first," he said, running his hand down over my throat and between my breasts. He set the belt down and reached inside his pocket. He pulled out what looked like a small pair of earrings. Then I realized what they were. I swallowed and licked my lips in anticipation.

"No more improvised tools," he said thickly. He pulled me to my feet and tugged my blouse from the waist of my skirt. Then he slid his warm hand under the silky fabric and cupped my breast in his palm, kneading it. "Your tits are perfection, Brynn."

He undid my long row of buttons patiently, then pulled the lace down over each nipple. My buds were rock-hard, and I closed my eyes as he flicked one, then the other, sending shockwaves down my body. I expected his warm, soft tongue to give me mercy, so I gasped when I was met with cold, ungiving metal as it cushioned and squeezed each nipple.

The pinch was exquisitely delicious, and the sensation ran the circuit of nerves all the way down to my clit, making it greedy with the need for relief.

The small clamps were a rich gold color, with black onyx decorative beads and little pearls hanging delicately from the end of the smooth, sleek metal. These were not the cheap nipple clamps I ordered online and used alone in my townhome. These were as gorgeous as any custom-made jewelry; how he'd gotten them so quickly after learning I worked here, all while busily taking over a new role, was beyond me.

I didn't question it, though. I just basked in the sweet pain as it rolled over me in waves.

He gave them a gentle tug, sending me to another plane of pleasure. Then he lifted the lace back over my breasts, covering the clamps, and buttoned my blouse back up for me. I reached for him, longing to touch his bare skin, but he grabbed my wrists before I could get to what I'd been aching to hold.

"Back on your knees."

I stared deep into his eyes, deciding whether to submit again or not. It was unlike me in every way. But there was something so appealing about Pierce's strong personality—about his sure demands. Maybe it was because I knew what pleasure awaited on the other side of his order.

And I knew it was everything I wanted.

I slowly lowered back down to my knees, his cock jutting out in front of me, taunting me.

"Take what you want now, beautiful," he said, stroking it.

I leaned forward, gently kissing the head of his cock and taking my time licking along his wide shaft. When I came back to the top and flicked my tongue over his opening, salty warmth met my lips. Then I slowly took him all the way into my mouth, moaning as he slid past my lips and down the warm tunnel of my throat. He let me set the pace, but I was greedy, hungry for more. As he gripped the back of my head, gently rocking his hips forward and feeding his cock into my mouth, I whimpered. I wanted so badly to touch myself as I sucked his beautiful shaft.

Without warning, Pierce gripped my arms and pulled me up to stand. We were both breathing heavy, wild with lust and needing release. He walked me slowly backward until we were at the end of the couch. Then he placed his hand between my shoulder blades and gently pressed my breasts forward until I was bending over its arm. His fingers teasingly ran over my bottom, lifting my skirt reverently over my backside before squeezing it.

"God, this ass of yours is going to be my downfall, Brynn."

I had no clue what was so special about my ass, but the fact that it made a man as powerful and sexy as Pierce go weak in the knees made me want to write songs about it.

"Don't move," he said. He walked back over to the table and picked up his belt, snapping the leather together as he doubled it over. The leather made an audible snap, and my pussy dripped in response.

He ran his hand over my backside again, kneading the soft flesh. "May I?" he asked, surprising me. "You aren't my sub, and I'm not a dom. I just love your fucking body. It inspires me to do all kinds of kinky things to it."

I swallowed, aroused at his honesty about his desire.

"I won't do anything you're not comfortable with. But man . . . I really want to smack that sweet ass of yours with this belt and watch it grow a rosy pink for me. Do you trust me, Brynn? To give you the kind of pain that brings pleasure too?"

Was I really considering letting him do this to me? I'd never let a man spank me with anything other than his hand before. But the sound of the leather snapping together had made my insides purr. I knew there was something more I was longing for—something that maybe the belt could give me. Whatever it was, I was certain Pierce would figure it out. And for some reason, I *did* trust him.

"Please," I whimpered, hot with need.

"Close your eyes, baby girl," he said, wrapping my hair around his fist and pulling my head back.

He ran his tongue sensually over my throat until he found my mouth, capturing it in his. His tongue pressed deep inside and danced with mine for what felt like ages; I surrendered to the sacred need we both seemed to have to consume one another.

"I'm ready," I whispered.

Pierce chuckled. "Yes, you are."

He pressed me back down to the couch and stood taller, running the belt slowly over the soft flesh of my ass to help me get comfortable with it. Then he slowly started tapping my ass, small swishes back and forth that were just enough to entice, but not sting. The movements were firm but gentle. Confident and controlled. Just when I thought I couldn't take anymore, he trailed his fingers along my slit, lightly wetting them before bringing them to his lips.

"Mmm," he said, drawing out the pleasurable moan, "an angel who tastes like heaven."

He squeezed my ass again and kneaded it with his strong fingers. "I'm going to give you one quick pass, Brynn. Your ass is far too beautiful to be leaving welts—that's not the kind of spanking I'm into, anyway. Next time, I'll use a leather flogger. That's what your pussy really wants. This," he said, lifting the belt and finally bringing it down across my ass, "is just foreplay."

"Fuck," I moaned when the leather met my skin. The impact took me by surprise, and I liked it. A lot. The sting was quick, but the lasting effect was a sensual burning that raged deep inside my core. He ran his flat palm over the tender spot and then gently massaged the soft flesh.

The next thing I knew, Pierce was on his knees, his face buried in my ass. His hands were everywhere, kneading my thighs and parting the mounds of my flesh to get his mouth even closer. He bathed me in kisses, plunging his tongue deep inside me to taste my arousal for him. There was nothing to grip on the smooth leather couch, and I couldn't hold it back any longer. The way his tongue worshipped me, slamming into me hard and fast, pushed me over the edge.

"Oh god!" I cried out as I soared—relief finally flooding through me. I pushed myself up with my hands, but my body, once again, felt decimated by him.

"You're going to have to learn to be quieter, Miss Hartley," he teased, pulling me into his arms. I was a ravaged, shaky mess, but I was satiated.

Guilt tore through me when I noticed that, at some point, Pierce had tucked his swollen cock back into his pants. The poor man had to be in pain from his raging hard-on.

"Let me return the favor." I teasingly ran my finger over the clasp on his dress slacks.

"I wish you could," he said sincerely. "But I didn't bring a condom. I thought we were going to meet at Havana's, and then I could bring you back to the hotel—where I have plenty."

"We still can," I said, hopeful.

"Why don't we finish talking first. I'll order some take-out, and we can have a real meeting. I obviously respect your position here, Brynn—beyond having you in my lap. And I don't want to minimize that just because I also want to fuck your brains out every chance I get."

I chuckled but then grew serious at the thought of shifting gears from being so deeply intimate one moment to being colleagues the next.

"I'm still not sure this is such a wise idea, Pierce."

In fact, I knew it was dangerous. I'd tried to mix business with pleasure before with my ex Nick. All it earned me was a broken heart when he backstabbed me for a promotion. And once someone broke my trust, it was over. That was my hard line in relationships, and his betrayal still stung. At least I didn't have to worry about seeing him around the office anymore. He was Penguin's problem now.

"It's fine, as long as it's consensual. We're both adults, and I think you're worth trying to figure out how to navigate all this," he said, pulling me in for a kiss.

I could taste myself on his lips.

"Can I be up-front with you about something?" he asked, entering our delivery order on an online app. "This is confidential, and I need to be able to trust you with what I'm about to say."

I nodded, grateful that I wasn't the only one having to do all the trusting around here. "Of course, Pierce. That's not who I am. If you tell me something in confidence, it stays between us."

He took a deep breath, shoving his hands in his pockets and looking devastatingly handsome. "I actually don't know how long I'll be here in this position, Brynn. It's more of a stopgap to help Carlisa out."

Wow. That was so not what I was expecting to hear.

"I can't disclose anything more than that right now, as a lot of things are still up in the air. As soon as I can, I promise I'll fill you in. But the important part for you to really understand is that I won't be your direct boss forever. You just had your annual review, so I won't be in charge of your career path or income. So, there's no downside to us getting to know each other better, is there?"

Well, that certainly changed things. It also gave me hope about my future at Sterling and Masters. But it also raised more questions than it answered.

"Either way, I'm not sure I can keep doing this," I said honestly. "I feel phenomenal whenever I'm with you. But I'm not exactly a 'keep it casual' type of girl. Saturday night really was a fluke for me. An amazing, cathartic, eye-opening, life-changing fluke. But I went into it knowing it was a one-night stand. Hoping it would be amazing sex but also understanding there were no strings attached. Once and done."

"Is that what you really want?" he asked, practically growling.

"I don't know what I want, Pierce. I'm terrified of getting my heart broken again. I'm scared of losing myself in you—because every time I'm around you, all I can think about is the sinful things I want you to do to my body. The ways I want you to push me. Corrupt me. Make me feel dirty and alive at the same time."

My heart was pounding.

Pierce was so achingly beautiful. More beautiful than any man had a right being. Could I really walk away from him and never let him touch me again? See him around the office and wonder if someone else was on her knees for him just a room away? The little green monster in me gnashed her teeth and bared her claws.

Oh, fuck no!

But there was a small part of me that hesitated—just the tiniest bit—because in less than a week, the boy I thought I once loved was coming back into town, all grown up. Seeing him online was one thing. But how would my body react when I got to hug him again? Not to mention my heart . . .

"We don't have to decide today," I said quietly.

"No, we don't. But I—"

Pierce never got a chance to finish his thought because a knock at the door let us know our food had arrived.

I left work that night full and hopeful—which was a much better end to my day than how it started. But I decided to take a rain check on going back to the hotel with him, and he was surprisingly understanding about the whole thing. I didn't know what our future was going to hold. All I knew was if I kept the door open with Pierce, there was probably going to be a flogger involved.

And that was definitely a silver lining.

That night I talked to my grampa on the phone. I asked him if he remembered Noah, but the name didn't ring a bell, which worried me. Babs said Sunday was another hard day for him. They were getting more and more frequent.

I hopped in the shower, needing to wash away the stress of my day. I laughed when I took off my lace bra and discovered my nipple clamps still firmly in place. My nipples were sore after wearing them for so long, so I gently massaged them back into shape. When I was toweled off and in my warm jammies, I made myself a cup of hot lemon water so I could snuggle in bed and read myself to sleep.

The doorbell caught me before I could make my way up to the bedroom. I looked at the clock on my phone. Who in the world was at my house at this time of night? I marched to the entryway and lifted the small vertical blinds beside the door so I could see who it was. To my surprise, it was Pierce's driver.

"Is everything okay?" I asked after opening the door.

"Yes, ma'am," he said politely. "I have some packages Mr. Abrams asked me to deliver to you tonight. He said it was urgent."

Urgent, my ass.

"Thank you—" I realized I didn't even know his name.

He must've seen my discomfort. "Harrison."

"Thank you, Harrison," I said, accepting the large, black shopping bags from him. "My, Mr. Abrams seems to have gone overboard."

He chuckled. "Yes, he's very generous."

"Well, please tell him I said thank you."

"I will. I have one more thing for you, Miss. I'll be right back."

I deposited the bags on the floor and turned just in time to see Harrison carrying my large, folded wings in his arms. I burst out laughing. "That's not something you see every day," I said.

"Indeed."

"Well, thank you again, Harrison. Please give Mr. Abrams my best."

The wink he gave me before he headed back to the car told me everything I needed to know. Why did I suddenly feel like Julia Roberts?

CHAPTER TWELVE

SHAY SCRUNCHED HER nose as she gave me the once-over in the elevator. I had to reach deep for Jesus in that moment. I could tell she wanted to say something snarky, but I was not going to open that door so easily for her.

"Do you have a special meeting or something?" she finally asked, unable to mind her own business.

"Why do you ask?"

She looked like she'd eaten something rotten or smelled a stinky fart. "Because you *never* wear suits, Brynn," she said, with an emphasis on the *duh* part of that statement.

"And your point?"

"Are you trying to suck up to the new boss?" she asked pointedly.

More like suck *off*, not suck up, I wanted to say just to shut her up.

"Are you trying to body shame me, Shay?" I asked. "Can't a woman wear whatever she wants, whenever she wants? And," I reminded her, turning tit for tat and sweeping my eyes over her casual outfit choice, "we do work in corporate America, in case you didn't get the memo."

The ding of the elevator was my salvation, and I couldn't get off the elevator fast enough. Despite her obvious issue with my outfit, I actually loved it. She was right—I didn't usually get this dressed up for work. But I felt *very* powerful and *very* sexy. And whether Pierce asked me to or not, I knew I would be making this look a staple in my wardrobe from here on out.

But, of course, Shay couldn't let it go that easily. She followed me to my office, talking the whole time. "You know you're not getting the executive editor position now, right, Brynn? I mean, with Mr. Abrams here, your shot is virtually nonexistent. There's no way Carlisa won't keep a man like that around when she gets back. She probably already has the CIO position and is just not saying anything yet. I mean, why else would she hire someone so capable if she was just going to let him go in six weeks? It doesn't make sense."

Well, she was right about one thing. It *didn't* make sense. I didn't have those answers, either, but I did have insider information thanks to Pierce. But I wasn't sharing that with her. I glanced toward his office and saw that the door was closed. It was nerve-wracking knowing he'd be on the other side of that door all day.

I turned toward Shay. "I'm not sure what your point is. But my career aspirations—and my wardrobe choices—are really none of your business. Now, if you'll excuse me, I have a ridiculously busy day."

I fell into my chair and pulled up my schedule. A meeting had been accepted on my behalf by Rhonda. I now had a one to three time slot with Pierce. I was about to text Lindy when she flew into my office, closed the door, and handed me my hot mocha.

"I got you extra whip today," she said.

God bless her.

"Where did you go yesterday?" I asked, taking a sip. "I could've used the heads-up."

"Sorry, babe. I had a hot date with Walter, and I was cutting it close as it was," she said.

"And where exactly was this hot da—whoa!" I finally noticed the enormous ring on her left hand. "Holy shit! Lindy!" I squealed, jumping up. I made my way around the desk and grabbed her hand. "Is that what I think it is?"

She was speechless for once, nodding as she looked down at the giant sparkler. When she looked back up at me, there were tears in her eyes.

I wrapped my arms around her. "I'm so happy for you!"

"I know. I can't believe it. I'm still in shock."

I pulled back and grabbed her hand again. "Fuck!" I whispered. "That man is seriously loaded."

I turned the ring this way and that. "What kind of rock is this?"

It was a pear-shaped diamond of some sort, with tiny diamonds around the main stone and two smaller pear-shaped diamonds on both sides. The setting itself was gold, but I couldn't tell what color the diamond actually was. It just glowed. From outer space. Because—did I mention—it was ginormous?

"He said it's a pink diamond, though it looks more like a pale rose gold to me."

"A pink diamond?" I sputtered. "Lindy, that's one of the rarest diamonds in the world."

"I know," she whispered. "He bought my ring in London this past summer. He worked with Kensington Parker on its design."

I whistled. "Do I dare ask how many carats this bad boy is?"

"Fourteen," she said quietly. "Well, that's for all the diamonds."

"Fourteen!" I practically screamed. "Do you know how much that thing had to cost?"

She bit her lip and nodded.

"I'm sorry. Am I making you uncomfortable?"

"No," she said, but I saw she had some reservation.

"What is it, then? Aren't you excited?"

"Oh my god, I'm over the moon!" she gushed. "I just—I'm not used to this kind of money, Brynn. Sure, I love being taken care of. I mean, that's one of the reasons why I love dating older, more experienced men to begin with. But this—this is going to be my life now. I can't wrap my head around it."

"Lindy," I said, "you love this man. Don't let the ring intimidate you. He hasn't changed. You haven't changed. It's just going to be an adjustment. But the marriage part? That doesn't freak you out even just a little bit?"

She laughed. "Not at all. I knew when I met Walter I was in trouble."

I grinned. "We're going to have to go out and celebrate one night this week!"

"I'd love that," she said, beaming.

"Has Dan seen it yet?"

She shook her head.

"Good luck with that when he does," I teased.

The knock at my door startled me. When I looked up, my heart skipped a beat. Pierce was standing there looking devastatingly handsome in a tailored black suit and a crisp white dress shirt. I waved for him to come on in.

"Did I miss the party?" he asked. "I heard some serious squealing going on over here."

I laughed. "I'm so sorry. It was completely my fault."

"That's okay. Just a good reminder that these walls are paper thin," he said and winked. "Did you get everything you needed for our one o'clock?"

My insides liquified, and I had to press my thighs tightly together.

"I have everything in order," I confirmed.

"Good. Well, I'll see you later," he said. "And Miss Westgate?"

"Yes, Mr. Abrams?"

"Congratulations," he said, nodding to her hand. "He has good taste."

She blushed furiously. "Thank you."

"Have a good morning."

Pierce shut the door, and I watched as he walked to his office, his eyes trained on mine the whole time.

"Jesus, Brynn!" Lindy hissed.

"What?" I asked, snapping my attention back to her.

"Are you fucking him in the office?"

"Wh—why would you ask that?"

"I *saw* the way you devoured each other with your eyes. And neither of you is as subtle as you think you are. You'd better be careful."

"What's the worst that could happen? He's not going to let me get fired. Someone smart told me that."

"How do you really *know* that, though? You're playing with fire."

"Yeah," I said, sighing. But the desire to be consumed by Pierce was greater than the fear of being burned. It was a very dangerous situation to be in.

"You're not going to stop, though, are you?"

It was my turn to bite my lip. "I don't know," I said. "I'm seeing Noah next Tuesday for our business meeting. But he asked me to meet him for dinner at his grandmother's estate on Wednesday. The one he's selling."

"As in a date?"

"As in two old friends getting together, is my take."

"But what *vibe* are you really getting?" she asked. She knew me too well.

"I feel like he's curious to see if we still have a connection. He asked to FaceTime this week, so we could catch up on a more personal level before our meeting. It would be kind of weird to jump right into business negotiations after not seeing each other for eighteen years."

"True. But is that all this is? What about Pierce?"

I shrugged. "I don't honestly know. I mean, that man in the office next door? He *does* things to me, Lindy, you know? But I can't tell if it's just because of the multiple orgasms and the huge—"

"Don't!" she said, putting her hand up and stopping me. "We're besties, so of course I *want* to know. But there are some things that might be better if I *don't* know about my new boss."

"Fair enough," I said.

"Christ!" she muttered, curiosity winning out. "How big?"

I used my hands to show her.

She groaned. "If I wasn't already engaged . . ."

I laughed.

"Just be careful, okay?" she said, getting serious. "I don't want to see you get hurt again."

Me either.

It was the last thing I was looking forward to in any of these scenarios. But with three hearts on the line, it was bound to happen to one of us.

~

THE MORNING FLEW by, and I was officially done with the Megan Morris manuscript. It was her best yet, and I cried at the end. It was a darling female/female rom-com, and the world really needed more of those. I sent her my style sheet and feedback, as well as the final Word doc with my edits, just in time to grab a quick snack and head into my one o'clock with Pierce.

I'd taken time to brush my teeth, freshen up my makeup, and calm my butterflies. But the minute I stood at his door, knocking like a schoolgirl at the dean's office, my jitters reappeared. I glanced over my shoulder at the pit. Everyone was heads-down busy, focusing on their work. I could see Dan talking on his phone in his office across the main floor. He lifted a distracted wave my way, then turned in his chair.

Then I saw Shay—and wouldn't you know it? She was walking my way. I groaned. *Hurry up, Pierce! Open the damn door.*

Three other women headed my way, too, and said hello. It was as if we were all waiting for the same thing. "Uh, what's going on?" I asked.

"Your guess is as good as ours," Quinn said, shrugging. "We got the same invite you did."

Huh?

I pulled out my phone to check my schedule. Sure enough, the first part of our meeting from one to two had multiple invitees. Somehow, in my excitement about being alone with Pierce, I'd overlooked that small detail.

I glanced around at the group and noticed one common theme: we were all the editors representing the romance genre at Sterling and Masters. I had contemporary and erotic romance. Quinn had historical and time-period. Shay had clean and inspirational romance. Kennedy had all things woo-woo: paranormal, dystopian, post-apocalyptic, sci-fi, fantasy, urban fantasy, and aliens. And Vega had multicultural and LGBTQ. Since Megan Morris's book had a female/female couple, it had gone to Vega first for a sensitivity read before coming to my desk for final edits.

My attention returned to the reason why we were all here, when the door opened and there stood Pierce, larger than life. My insides turned to goo at the memory of him taking a belt to my backside in this very office just yesterday. As we shuffled in, he said, "Take a seat, everyone. Brynn, why don't you grab the seat by the window? The leather chair is mine."

Christ. He wanted me to sit in the same place where he'd bent me over yesterday. My knees nearly buckled. Everyone else walked in and took their seats, Shay sitting right next to where I'd be on the sofa.

Pierce placed a hand on my lower back after closing the door and led me to the conversation area. "I really need to get a conference room table in here," he said. "Brynn, would you mind asking Rhonda to order me one? I trust you can pick one out to match?"

I swallowed. All eyes were on me. Why would he ask me to do that? All I could do was nod. "Of course, Mr. Abrams."

He took off his suit jacket and rolled up his shirt sleeves before sitting down in a new chair directly next to me. It was larger than the other two conversation chairs and clearly meant for the king of the room. It fit Pierce perfectly.

"Thanks for meeting with me this afternoon. Let's start with formalities and get them out of the way. First of all, call me Pierce. Mr. Abrams is my father. I don't like being Mr. Abrams in the office unless it's to crush my competition," he said, grinning.

"I talked to a few of you yesterday, but I'd like to go around and get the elevator speech about who you are, how long you've been here, what you're working on—that sort of stuff."

"Is this going to be replacing our weekly romance editors staff meeting?" Shay asked.

"We'll talk more about that later," Pierce promised. "For now, I just need a quick handle on workload, experience, priorities, projections. That kind of thing. Why don't you start?"

Shay swallowed, looking more nervous than I'd seen her in a while. "Well, the clean romance line is going strong. I've had a lot of submissions from literary agencies that are scrambling to rehome several of their authors after RMG closed its doors."

"RMG?" he asked.

"Revelations Media Group. I handle clean romance, inspirational fiction, and religious fiction."

"I see. And RMG focuses on one religion specifically, correct?"

"Yes, the Christian reader base."

"And how many authors are you looking to take on?"

"I haven't done a full analysis yet, sir," she said.

How could I want to slap her so badly when she was sitting there talking about Christian romance? I was surely going to hell. But hearing the word "sir" come from her lips while talking to Pierce? Next-level jealousy flooded over me. If anyone was going to be calling him that, it was me.

"I want a proposal by end of day on what percentage of your work is religious versus clean romance versus inspirational fiction. I also want brief bios of the authors in each segment and how many new authors you have capacity to take on with RMG closing."

"Yes, sir," she said, crossing her legs and looking at him with her big doe eyes.

I clutched my leather-bound notepad and screamed inside.

We went around like that covering all the genres until he got to me. I gave him a quick update about my work and what percentage was contemporary versus erotica or steamy romance—it was a sixty-five/thirty-five split. I also gave him a breakdown of the authors I had, who I was looking to pull in, and our projected growth in the contemporary category over the next six months.

"I also have an opportunity I'd like to discuss with you privately," I said, thinking of Eve Donohue. I needed to explain some things first. "I have a pitch meeting set for next Tuesday with a very influential international literary agency who is representing a unique client and wants to get a proposal in front of us. At first blush, I think it's one we'll want to jump on. We have first right of refusal, and that's only going to be the case for a small window of time—possibly a day."

"Interesting," he said. He looked at me with a new appreciation in his eyes now that we were really talking business. "And how did that come about?"

I cleared my throat. "Connections, *sir*."

"I see," he said. He was holding a stack of papers, held together with a fat binder clip identical to the ones he'd used on me in the hotel room. The man was pure evil. He handed one of the printouts to each of us.

I was confused because it was an organizational chart, but not for our company. The tasks were similar, but the workflow and reporting structure were completely different. While we all studied the chart, I heard Pierce playing with the binder clip. I snuck a peek at him from the corner of my eye, and he winked at me, tossing me the clip.

I fumbled to catch it before anyone else noticed.

"This is going to be the new romance division," Pierce said. "No names have been filled in for any of these roles because we'll be doing an audit of everyone's current workload, capacity, and financial revenue contributing to the overall genre."

The group looked completely stunned.

I had so many questions. "Will this new division be reporting to you still?"

"It will. We're just condensing touch points and optimizing workflow through one official division lead per genre. Every group is going through this streamlining and restructuring process. The new romance division executive editor will have more responsibilities as well, so it's unlike any one person's current role here."

I nodded, excited about the potential this new role created.

"Will this position be open for applications?" Shay asked. It was what we were all thinking.

"No," Pierce said. "I'll be announcing the new executives for each division tomorrow in our staff meeting. Those top talents have already been identified and are being notified today."

I swallowed. *Well, shit.* Why didn't he give me a heads-up about this yesterday when he was talking about all these "big changes" coming? Then I realized why. *Because, stupid. He's fucking you. He doesn't need your approval to make important business decisions. It's* his *role now. Not yours.*

Still. It stung.

"That's all," he said. "If you have any questions, please send them to my PA, Alastor. You haven't met him yet, but he's been cc'd on all my communications, so you have his email address. He'll be starting in person at this office tomorrow. Rhonda will continue handling other division-wide responsibilities, but he's my personal executive assistant and will have access to my schedule. He'll also be your first point of contact for getting in touch with me."

We all stood to leave, everyone visibly shaken.

"Miss Hartley," he said, "could you please stay a moment?"

Crap.

I looked around at the others. Jealousy was reflected back at me in one set of eyes in particular.

"Sure," I said warily.

"I'd like an immediate update on that potential deal you were telling me about," he clarified. "It sounds like we may need to pull in some other teams to make things happen if it's the level of opportunity you suggest."

I saw relief wash over Shay's face before she followed the other women out. Pierce locked the door behind them, drew the shades, and then used the intercom to contact Rhonda.

"I'm in a critical developmental meeting with Miss Hartley and am not to be disturbed for any reason."

"Yes, Mr. Abrams."

He hung up the phone, then stalked toward me. Pierce cupped the back of my head and immediately crushed his mouth down on mine. I dropped my padfolio to the floor and wrapped my arms around his neck, pressing my body against his.

He tasted manly and minty and soothingly familiar already.

"Fuck, Brynn," he groaned quietly in my ear. "Do you have any idea how hard it was for me to see you come in this morning in this outfit and keep my mind on work?"

I laughed, arching my neck as he kissed his way down my throat. "And whose fault is that, Mr. Abrams?" I purred. "Thank you, by the way. This was all too extravagant."

"It was purely for selfish reasons," he said. "Did you do what I asked?"

I nodded, my hands playing with the back of his hair. "I can't wait to show you later," I said quietly. "Is the offer still open to go back to the hotel with you after work?"

"Yes," he said, "but you're deluding yourself if you really think I can wait that long to taste you."

I looked up at him with widened eyes. It was one thing to fool around after-hours when most everyone else had already gone home. It was another thing altogether when there was a floor full of associates just one door away.

"I am *not* showing you what I'm wearing right now," I hissed between clenched teeth.

He lowered his hand down my leg, then up under my tight pencil skirt and over my backside. He'd felt the garter belt on his way up and grinned wickedly. "That's my good girl," he said. "You deserve to be rewarded, don't you think?"

He massaged my ass as he kissed me again, and I couldn't think straight. He walked me backward toward his desk as we kissed, his mouth gently exploring mine. He had a way of maneuvering me until he got what he wanted, and as my ass hit his desk, I knew there was no way I would be able to talk him out of this. What Pierce wanted, Pierce seemed to get when it came to my body. I had zero willpower where he was concerned.

He slowly peeled my blazer off, his eyes lighting with approval when he saw my silky, pale blue blouse. I'd worn the nipple clamps again—just into his office, though. They were too painful to keep on all day, but I knew he could see them through the blouse. He cupped my breasts and rubbed them, gently tugging the clamps to make me squirm with desire.

"Tell me what you thought about when you got dressed this morning," he said, turning me around. "Put both of your hands on the desk and answer my question."

I could hardly remember the question I was so turned on.

He lifted my pencil skirt until it was around my waist, and he moaned as he eyed my lingerie. I'd worn the lacy, black garter belt and stockings he'd sent over. I'd never worn anything like this before, but I had to admit, I felt sexier than I ever had—especially knowing it turned Pierce on.

"Well?" he asked, sliding a hand up over my thigh and between my legs. "Part your legs for me, Brynn."

Though it was unlikely anyone could see into the office building and all the way back to his desk, I was nervous about having the blinds on the windows wide open. There was something so risky and taboo about it. Yet, I couldn't seem to resist Pierce.

I parted my legs and placed my hands on his desk like he asked me to. Correction—like he'd ordered me to. I shivered with anticipation.

"Honestly?" I said as he slid his fingers back and forth between my legs. "I thought about this. About you tasting me again, like you did yesterday. But I imagined we'd be at the hotel, not here in the office."

"Well, if you can be a good girl and be quiet, then no one will have to know," he said, sliding two fingers inside me.

I whimpered as he moved them back and forth.

"Later tonight, you're going to take everything else off except for the garter belt, stockings, and heels. Then I'm going to fuck your brains out, Brynn Graceland Hartley. Over every square inch of that hotel room."

My heart accelerated. Of course he knew my middle name. He had access to my personnel files. Still. It sounded sexier than sin coming from his mouth.

"God, yes," I said, nearly panting.

"But first, I need just a taste of you to hold me over."

I felt him loop my black silk panties over his thumbs and shivered as he pulled them down my legs. Then he lifted one of my legs at the knee and brought it up to the desk, leaving me splayed wide open.

"Are you positive the door is locked?"

"Of course," he said. I heard him tear open a condom but didn't know what was coming next. Part of the fun with Pierce was the element of surprise and his adventurous nature. I needed both in my sexual partners.

He leaned over my back, and I turned my head, letting him capture my mouth in a sinfully slow and decadent kiss. He slid his fingers back inside me and curled them a few more times, nearly bringing me to the edge. He pulled his fingers out before I could come and brought them to his mouth.

"Shh," he said, his breath hot and musky. "Remember, these walls are thin."

I was so insanely turned on I didn't realize why he'd said that until I felt the thick head of his cock breach my lips as he pushed all the way inside of me. I clutched the edge of his desk and bit the inside of my cheek to stop myself from screaming out his name.

Pierce gripped my waist and slowly rolled his hips, lodging himself so deep inside of me he practically lifted my feet from the floor each time he thrust to the hilt. It was hard, slow, and demanding. I had to curl my toes inside my pumps to keep them on, and my insides burned with an eternal, aching need.

"Pierce," I begged as quietly as I could. This was not fair.

He pulled me off the desk, his cock still buried inside me. "Fuck, Brynn."

He looped his arms under mine, bending his elbows so he was holding me by the shoulders against him. "I'm sorry. I promised myself I wouldn't do this until we got back to the hotel room, but I couldn't wait. You're driving me to distraction."

Now was not the time to remind him that this was his idea.

"I can't get enough of you," he growled, his voice low and thick. He increased his speed, and I gripped his forearms as he drove himself in and out of me at an unrelenting pace. "Fuck, fuck, fuck!" he gasped hoarsely as he pounded into me.

I was so close to coming. His cock was rubbing against my G-spot, and I was nearly delirious with arousal. As if sensing this, he reached his hand down and rubbed my clit furiously. It took no time for that to push me right over. I closed my eyes, bursts of white light short-circuiting my brain and exploding behind my lids as I came. My body spasmed with each last pass of his fingers. I was gripping the back of his head now, falling against his chest as he slowly walked my body down from its orgasm.

"That's it," he murmured in my ear, and he kissed my neck and earlobe. "God you're a sight to see when you come. A fucking sex goddess, Brynn."

He slowed the rubbing of my clit as he brought me back to the desk.

"Bend back over," he said, so I did. I gripped the desk and prepared myself for what was coming. I knew the pace he'd have to set so he could come. I lifted my knee onto the smooth, wooden surface and arched back, knowing what he desired. Pierce growled, using one hand to grip my shoulder and the other to hold my forearm. Then he fucked me. Hard.

I bit the inside of my cheek so painfully I was afraid I was going to make it bleed. How we remained any level of quiet I had no idea, though leaving his pants on certainly helped buffer the sound of our bodies slapping together.

His grunting grew more frantic, and I thought Pierce might be the one who was going to blow our cover. "Fuck!" he hissed after a few more pounding thrusts. He tightened his grip around my bicep and came. Then his body relaxed and he slumped over, kissing me everywhere—on my face, my shoulder, my back—before pulling out. I stood and straightened my skirt, then looked around for my underwear. Pierce grinned and held them up by a finger. I reached for them, but he shook his head and quietly slid them into his pants pocket.

Well . . . shit.

I ran my fingers through my long brown hair and shook it out, then I put my blazer back on while I watched Pierce dispose of the condom and then zip himself up. The man was certifiably going to be the death of me.

He said nothing, just wrapped me in his arms and held me for the longest time. I relaxed against his chest and let myself be held. It was a nice feeling to experience with Pierce after all the heat and intensity.

"Brynn, I need you to know something."

"Hmm?" I said in a satisfied stupor. I felt like a cat being petted and loved on, and I wanted more.

"I've never done this before."

"Done what?"

"Slept with someone who worked for me. Fucked someone in my office. Dated anyone I worked with."

Dated?

It didn't mean we were, it just meant he never had.

"I appreciate you telling me that."

"I just didn't want you to think this was my MO or something."

I chuckled. "I was beginning to wonder. You seem to have this whole sneaking-sex-in-during-the-workday thing down pat."

"I can't help it, Brynn. You bring out the beast in me."

"I like that," I said, grinning.

"Yeah, I think you do," he said into my hair as he nuzzled me. "I think you like that maybe a little too much."

"Speaking of which," I hinted, "are we still on for later?"

He laughed. "You're incorrigible."

"I think you mean *insatiable*," I said breathily.

He bent down to kiss me as I looked up at him. He nibbled my lower lip. "That too."

"Am I ever going to get my underwear back?"

"Hell no," he said with a laugh before he pulled back. "I'm going to take these out all day long and smell you, angel."

"Christ, Pierce," I said. "How am I going to concentrate thinking about that?"

"If I have to suffer a slow and torturous death, you do too."

"Fine," I said. "But when I have to play with myself in my office because my private parts are rubbing together all day, I'm going to text you the play by play."

"You wouldn't."

"Watch me."

He grinned. "My perfect match," he said, kissing my

forehead. "Hey, before you leave, I actually do still need to talk with you about work. Have a few minutes?"

I checked my phone and nodded. We had about forty-five minutes until the "meeting" was supposed to be over. "What is it?" I asked. "Did you really want me to order you a small conference room table for in here?"

"I do, actually. I want you to pick one out that you want to be fucked on. That's my only criteria."

Sweet. Baby. Jesus.

"Come," he said, grinning as he took my hand. "Let's sit down and go over a few things. I have something to run by you."

For the next thirty minutes we talked shop, and I was fascinated by the way Pierce's brain worked and how much he seemed to know about the industry. His ambition was sexy as fuck, but sexier than that was the way he made connections beyond the editing arm of Sterling and Masters and could see the bigger publishing landscape and trends. It was nice to talk about work again with someone I was attracted to. It was something I missed after losing Nick. He understood the pressures that came with editing and publishing.

The only thing he hadn't understood? How to be loyal.

Not with me, and certainly not with work.

"So, tell me some more about this opportunity you mentioned earlier," Pierce said.

"Well, an old friend of mine works for Chance and Chambers Creative out of London. He represents Eve Donohue—"

"Whoa," Pierce said.

"I know, right? Well, apparently, she's created a new twelve-book contemporary romance series that her London publisher isn't interested in. They want her to stay in her magical realms lane. I mean, I get it. It's how people know her. It's what made her millions. But that doesn't mean she can't write romance."

"I understand the hesitancy, though. Does she want to use a pen name? Or is she willing to publish under Donohue?"

"I don't know yet. I'm meeting with Noah Chance on Tuesday to hear the series pitch. He sent me the first book in the series—it's based on the zodiac signs and how they play into the characters' relationships."

"Interesting. Do you buy in to all that stuff?"

I paused. "I do, actually."

"What's your sign?"

"Scorpio."

"Which means *what* exactly?"

"Uh—the good traits or the bad?"

"There are no bad traits, Brynn. Every human needs all the quirks they were born with, to make them unique and complete. You can't have nothing but sunshine and rainbows. There's a reason that saying is a cliché. The light can't shine without the contrast of the darkness."

"I get that better than anyone," I said. "I can be moody and stubborn. Ambitious and strategic. I crave depth and intelligence. None of this shallow shit for me. Let's see. I'm loyal to a fault, until you cross me. Then I'm done. And when I'm done, I mean I'm *done*.

"I'm intuitive, observant, assertive, competitive, jealous. But I'm a good friend. And despite being emotional and deep, I also need a partner with a good sense of humor. Someone who can balance me out and make me laugh. Oh," I said, batting my eyelashes at him, "and Scorpios are also known for their intense sensuality."

"You don't say."

"We need partners who are experimental in the bedroom. Who are spontaneous and bring a little creativity."

"I'm up for the challenge," Pierce said, laughing. "What's the downside, as you say?"

"In case you missed it, I can be moody and stubborn. Scorpios are typically dominating and assertive—which isn't always a bad thing. But it can be when they're with another fixed sign," I admitted. "We're the quintessential enigma. A lot of people think we're hard to get close to, and even harder to read. And, in some cases, I think I can be a little like that until you really get to know me."

"I don't know. I've gotten pretty close to you," he said, winking.

"To my body," I pointed out. "What do you know about *me?*"

He grew quiet.

"Exactly."

"Let's change that, then," he said.

I looked into Pierce's vivid blue eyes. "What do you have in mind?"

"Let's start with a proper date, where we can actually talk. Which means out in public. Because I'm a weak man around you, and I'll be too tempted to get lost inside you again if it's in the hotel room."

A date? Did I really want that?

"I thought we were keeping things strictly physical."

"*I* never agreed to that," he said before adeptly switching the subject. "So, if you're a Scorpio, what am I?"

I hated to admit that I already knew what sign he was. "A Leo."

"And you know this how?"

"Uh, Lindy?"

Pierce laughed. "She's a good friend."

"She is. She needed to vet you first," I said. "For Lindy, that's a full astrological compatibility assessment."

"Did I pass?"

"Well, you're a fixed sign, like I am. Which means you're reliable like me. But also stubborn, strong-willed, and determined."

"Sounds about right." He chuckled. "What else do you see in me?"

"Leos are fire signs. Big energy," I said. "Natural leaders. Confident. Strong. Creative. They can be playful and spontaneous. Loyal. Romantic. They're known for their huge hearts and are generally very charismatic."

I ran my eyes over his face, trying to read his reaction. "I know this all sounds woo-woo. But there's a lot that factors into astrology, and a sliver of truth behind all the stereotypes."

"I'm sure there is. You seemed to nail me dead-on," he admitted. "So, tell me . . . what are the bad traits associated with Leos?"

"There are no bad traits, remember?"

He grinned. "She learns fast."

"Fine. Leos can be arrogant," I said pointedly. "Jealous. Headstrong. Demanding."

"I thought you were going to name the bad traits," he said.

I chuckled. "Did I mention egotistical?"

He inched closer to me on the couch. "How do we rate as lovers, though? Can I keep up with Miss Hartley's demanding needs?"

I swallowed, my mouth running dry. "Generally speaking, Leos are fiery and passionate. They have big hearts and are protective. So, if you have a Leo who loves you, they tend to protect your heart. They want to be the center of their partner's world and will do anything to please and take care of them. You know—that generous heart of theirs."

"And does any of that scare you?"

I considered his question. Did it really matter? I mean, if we were keeping things purely about sex, what did it matter what I felt about his light and his shadows?

"Nothing really scares me. I've been to my depths and back again. I've witnessed them in myself, so I know how to hold that space for others to work through. That being said, I've been hurt pretty badly in the past, so I don't give my heart over so easily anymore. But when I do, it's gone forever."

"Well," he said, "I guess now I have a goal."

My heart seriously wasn't ready for the likes of Pierce Abrams.

CHAPTER THIRTEEN

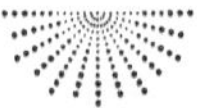

THE REST OF the day flew by fast. I found the desk I wanted and sent the link to Rhonda and Pierce for approval. It was a sleek, black Italian design with an oak and metal base. The best part was that the surface was high gloss, and I'd be able to see Pierce's reflection as he debased me on top of it. Goose bumps ran up and down my arms as I considered the possibilities.

That afternoon, just before five, I boldly sent Pierce a picture of my inner thigh beneath my pencil skirt and reminded him it was his fault I was having to scratch an itch during a workday. Two minutes later there was a knock on my office door.

I hadn't meant to tempt him into coming over to my office. I truly hadn't. I mostly wanted to drive him mad with desire until we could get back to his hotel room.

But he barged in, made me close the file I was working on, shut and locked my door, and then drew my blinds without asking me. Without saying another word, he crossed the room, spun my desk chair around, lifted my skirt, fell to his knees, and buried his face in my pussy. It was the single hottest thing a man had ever done, and I was a goner.

I held his head to my aching clit, my legs shaking as he latched on and wouldn't let go. He never touched the rest of me, didn't even put his fingers inside of me. He just wrapped his mouth around my clit and sucked the fuck out of it until I was coming all over his tongue.

Then he stood up, yanked me to my feet, and kissed me. I tasted myself on his tongue. On his warm, swollen lips. I was dizzy with lust when he took my hand and held it over his pants. He was swollen there too.

"This is what you do to me, Brynn. I could drive my cock through a brick wall right now, I'm so hard."

"Let's go back to your hotel, then," I said breathlessly.

"No," he growled.

I was confused.

He ran his hand through his thick brown hair, pacing the office. "I have something I need to talk with you about first. I was on my way over before I got that distracting little photo of yours."

Oops.

"Then after that, I'm taking you for dinner and music at a quiet little restaurant I love."

"O-kay," I said, drawing out the *O.*

He pointed to my chair. "Sit."

I adjusted my skirt, making sure it was pulled all the way down. I'd give anything for a washcloth right about now. My thighs were sticky with my arousal, which was both uncomfortable and a bit of a turn-on.

"Let me first say that this has nothing to do with our sexual relationship."

Oh god. Was I being fired?

"I know you were hoping for my position, and I'm truly sorry that you didn't get it. But Sterling and Masters is restructuring the organization anyway. And the position as Carlisa had it is technically going away. Carlisa has already put in her resignation. She knew before the baby was born that she wasn't coming back, but she'd never come right out and admit that."

So, the gossip mill was right on that one. I'd have to update the editorial team and see who won the pool.

"The long and short of it is that you are extremely qualified for any position you want at Sterling and Masters. I've looked at your performance reports over the last seven years, and I admire how you've not only grown but stretched yourself with your goal-setting and deliverables."

"Thank you," I said, sincerely flattered that he'd done that. "But I thought you said you wouldn't be in charge of my performance reviews and pay."

"I said *directly,*" he explained. "And I meant long-term."

"Okay."

"So, after meeting with the executive leadership team, we would like to offer you a promotion with the new title of Romance Editorial Executive. For now, you will continue to report to me. However, it also means that Kennedy, Vega, and Quinn will report to you now, starting tomorrow."

What?

"That's awfully fast. What if I said no?"

"Why would you do that, Brynn? This is an amazing opportunity to get some of the experience you were looking for when you wanted Carlisa's role. You'll be leading a small team. And this will set you up nicely for future advancement."

"I didn't *say* no," I clarified. "You were just awfully confident I would say yes."

He looked me square in the eyes. "I *get* you, Brynn. I know what motivates you. I know your ambition. You and I are a lot alike."

I nodded. He was right.

"I assume there will be a salary increase, since I'll be taking on more responsibility?"

He smiled. "It's a 20 percent increase, with the possibility of an annual bonus of up to 20 percent of your base salary, contingent on performance."

"How long do I have to decide?"

"Till the morning. I'd like to make the announcement in the staff meeting tomorrow."

"Who else is getting a promotion like this?" I asked.

"Dan, for one," he said. Then he outlined the new organizational chart reporting up to him, and things started to make a lot more sense. "So, you'll be partnering with Dan, Lindy, Jin, and Sayyid at a leadership level. Those will be your peers, and you'll all report to me for now. Our weekly staff meetings after tomorrow will be just the six of us. Then you'll decide how to manage your own team and how often to meet."

I nodded, already knowing my answer.

"Shay won't be happy about this," I said quietly. "There's a history between us that I think you need to know about first."

"I don't actually. Unless you'd like to share it for personal reasons. If you recall, I said that Kennedy, Vega, and Quinn will all be reporting to you."

I gaped at him. "What about Shay?"

"She's being terminated first thing in the morning. I'm not privy to discuss the specifics, but between you and me, there's a history of willful misconduct and a breach in her confidentiality agreement."

Well, shit. I knew why *I* didn't like Shay, but I didn't realize her toxicity bled over into her performance. "Let me guess," I said. "Does this have anything to do with Nick Reyes?"

"Some of it. How did you know? That's in a closed HR file."

"Nick is my ex," I explained. "Remember how I said that when I'm done, I'm done? Well, let's just say I found out that Nick had no loyalty to me and no loyalty to Sterling and Masters. And Shay was a big part of why. I just didn't have evidence that their deceit together went beyond the bedroom."

"Are you over him?" he asked. "He's made quite the name for himself in his new role."

"After what he did to me, Pierce . . . He broke my trust in every way imaginable, with the one person he knew it would cut the deepest with. He's dead to me."

Pierce nodded. "Understood. And remind me to never piss you off."

I smiled, but nothing about this part of the conversation made me happy. Sure, I hated Shay. But to this day, she didn't know I knew about her affair with my ex. She just hated me because I'd been there first. But learning that her betrayal went even deeper with Sterling and Masters, well, that just infuriated me. It was bad enough that Nick had crossed us. Now he would be in good company—two peas in a pod. Well, good riddance. He could have her.

"Will I be able to hire a replacement?"

"Are you saying yes?"

"I am," I said, grinning. "I accept."

A smile broke out across his face. "Then let's go celebrate!"

~

INSTEAD OF HAVING Harrison pick us up from the office, I drove my "new" Rolls-Royce. Pierce got a kick out of the old car and the stories I shared with him about my grampa. Over dinner we talked and shared more stories, and I got a much better glimpse at Pierce beyond the alpha male he was at work—and in the bedroom. I was discovering that he had a generous heart and playful personality.

We laughed over dinner and then took dessert to go. We acted like teenagers on a first date as I drove him around the city, giving him a sightseeing tour. I took him to several of the best murals in Charlotte—ones I suspected he'd enjoy too. We totally hammed it up and took pictures of ourselves in front of Thor, the technicolor portal, the Carolina Panthers, the confetti hearts (or what I called the "be kind" wall), and our most famous—the angel wings at Max and Lola's.

Then he surprised me, getting us into the Panthers' stadium, where we sat in the empty bleachers and ate a shared piece of key lime pie. The Panthers had just won their Sunday game and were gearing up for their Thursday night win—and they *would* win. The stadium was empty now, though. And my favorite part? Getting to go onto the field and toss a football around. I had to take off my heels for that, and I was pretty sure I ruined the expensive stockings he'd sent me. But it was worth every moment.

It was late by the time I pulled up to the hotel. I was a little disappointed when, instead of inviting me up to his room, Pierce got out of the convertible and walked over to the driver-side window. He leaned over and kissed me more tenderly than he ever had before.

"Sweet dreams, angel," he said before tapping the side of the door and heading into the Lion's Den.

It was too late to call my grampa by the time I got home, but I texted Babs and asked if they could meet me for lunch the next day. I had a lot of exciting news I wanted to share with him.

I showered and headed into my bedroom with a towel wrapped around my hair and my vanity bathrobe on—the most expensive thing I'd ever bought myself. Simply called "The Robe," it was something I saw on Goop and knew I had to have it right away. The white, belted bathrobe was simple, elegant, sexy, and completely worth every penny of its $250 price tag. Hey, it was better than the seventy-five dollar "This Smells Like My Vagina" candle I could've bought instead.

Note to self: Buy said candle for Lindy's engagement party.

Second note to self: Throw Lindy an engagement party.

As I was towel-drying my hair, I heard the distinctive ring of an incoming FaceTime call. I hopped onto my bed and answered the video call while brushing out my hair, assuming it was Pierce.

"Holy mother of god, Brynn," I heard. "You turned into a knockout."

I glanced at the screen, not recognizing the voice. Then I saw him. The boy next door. And my world tilted on its axis.

CHAPTER FOURTEEN

I GAPED IN DISBELIEF. I wanted to reach my fingertips out and touch my phone screen. I bit my lip, unable to catch my breath. He was more than breathtaking. He was real. Rugged. Sexy.

"Hey, pigtails," he said, winking.

I was speechless. For once in my life, I was actually speechless.

We sat there taking each other in for the longest time. The silence wasn't awkward, though. It was *us.* After all this time, it was as if we were still those kids living next door to one another. Gone was his towhead, but he still had a few freckles I could probably connect by memory. And though his hair was styled much different now—shaved on the sides, and fuller but swooped back on the top—it was still *my Noah* staring back at me.

"Noah," I finally said with a sigh, a genuine smile taking over.

"Brynnie." His new, deeper voice did things to me. It was a little raspy, a little thick. Like something that would roll across my skin and leave its mark forever.

"I'm glad you called before Tuesday," I said quietly. Suddenly, a week seemed like an eternity.

"I couldn't wait," he said. "How has so much time gone by?"

I shook my head, my fingers going to my lower lip as if I'd find the answers there. "What time is it in London?" I asked, snuggling into my comforter.

"Five thirty," he answered. He, too, was in bed.

"Did you get up just to call me?"

"No," he said softly. "I couldn't go to sleep. I've been thinking of you all night."

"Noah—"

"Just talk to me," he said.

"What do you want to talk about?"

"Remember that time when we tried to skateboard down our street together?"

"How could I forget? It was my first and last skateboarding lesson: Never try riding one down a hill tandem."

"Do you still have the scar on your leg?"

It was high on my upper, outer thigh.

"I do," I said, absently running my fingers over it now.

"Have any pets?"

"No," I said. "Though I saw a YouTuber who did a song about having six cats, and now it's all I can think about."

"I have a cat," he said.

"What kind is it?"

"I don't know. The cat kind? She's fluffy and orange. Has long fur."

"Sounds cute."

"She is."

"What's her name?"

"Pigtails."

Oh.

"Noah—"

"Don't," he pleaded. "I just need to hear your voice. You can't even imagine how much I've missed you over the years."

"I can, actually."

He grinned—it was infectious. "Cool."

"So . . . what kinds of things do you like to do these days?"

"Oh, you know. Same kind of stuff as when I was a kid—just with more expensive toys."

"Oh yeah? Like what?"

"Well, I race bikes now."

"Motorbikes?"

"No. Bicycles. Don't you remember how I lived on mine?"

"I do," I said, remembering his black mountain bike. "You were the one who got me into riding, remember? I was terrified the first time I went down our hill."

"Yeah, but it wasn't long before you were letting go of the handlebars and flying like a pro."

My eyes lit with the memory. "It felt *exactly* like flying," I marveled. "I still ride, you know. Nothing like what you do, from the sounds of it. But I get my miles in each week. Do the Queens College Booty Loop religiously."

Noah laughed. "Still plenty of good booty on the loop?"

"You know it!" I said, chuckling that the whole city knew about a bike route specifically named after the tushies of all the fit college students and other runners who shared the roads. Booties or not, it was still my favorite scenic route because of the mammoth trees that canopied the roads in the Myers Park area. "So, what kind of racing are you doing these days? You still on a mountain bike?"

"Nah, I upgraded that a long time ago," he said. "Ever heard of the Tour de France?"

"Get out."

"Yep. I was a sprinter for my team."

"That's hot," I said, wondering who he rode for and whether his team's yellow jersey contender had won.

"It's not so hot when you have to take a piss while you're riding but you can't stop because you have to get your rider to the finish line." He chuckled, little dimples I didn't remember framing his full lips.

"Ew," I said. "Maybe something I didn't need to know."

"We never held anything back, Brynnie."

"No, we didn't. It's what I loved about you."

"Loved? As in past tense? Ouch."

"You know what I mean."

"No, I don't, Brynn. I loved you then. You were my best friend. And I'll love you till the day I die. We made a blood oath, remember?"

The night he was talking about came rushing forward, and I almost got dizzy from the memories flooding me.

"How could I forget? It was our last night together. We snuck out at two in the morning and went down to your boat. It was August, so the cover was still off, but it was raised out of the water. We climbed in the back and listened to music on your little hand-cranked survival radio—remember that thing?"

"I still have it," he said, laughing.

"You do not!"

"I do, actually. Remember those god-awful bologna sandwiches I made us?"

"Ugh!" I said, groaning. "They had so much mustard on them!"

He full-on belly laughed. "We threw them in the lake for the fishes, and even they wouldn't eat them! They just floated there all sad and soggy in the water."

I laughed. "And the stars," I said, remembering the evening well. It had been etched into my heart like a celestial navigation map—one that often circled back to Noah over the years. "There was a meteor shower that night, which is why we snuck out to begin with."

"That's not *entirely* true."

When I didn't say anything, he did. "Remember? Operation Goodbye."

Oh, that. He was really going to go there.

"I remember," I said quietly.

"We decided that nothing could keep us apart. Not our parents. Not an ocean. Not the world. So, we promised that one day, we would find each other again—"

"*If* it was meant to be," I reminded him.

"If it was our destiny. And we sealed it with a blood oath. Do you remember that?"

"How could I forget? You stabbed my finger with a fishing lure!"

"I stabbed my own too," he reminded me.

"And then we mixed our blood finger to finger."

"Then we each licked our fingertips, and . . . ?" he trailed off, waiting for me to finish.

"And then you kissed me," I said, my eyes on his. They were a light hazel with warm brown flecks. I saw my past in there. But what scared me more was that I could also see a future. It felt like mine for the taking. But I was nowhere near ready to do something like that yet.

"It was a long time ago, Noah. Eighteen years is a lifetime away."

He studied me, then his eyes crinkled. "Doesn't feel that long, though, does it? We're still connected."

"Maybe," I said quietly.

"Maybe? Come on, pigtails. You telling me you aren't curious?"

The words slammed into me. That's what I'd told Pierce the night we hooked up. *I'm curious now.* Look where that got me.

I don't know why, but it suddenly felt wrong—like I was cheating. It was stupid. I wasn't dating Pierce. I didn't owe him anything. I could *talk* to an old friend.

But even I was calling myself out on my own BS.

Admit it, Brynn. You have feelings for them both.

"I need to get some sleep, Noah. I have an important meeting tomorrow morning."

"Oh yeah? Anything fun?"

"I was promoted today, actually."

"Congrats! That's awesome. Can I take you out to celebrate next week?"

"Well, I'm already seeing you Wednesday evening for dinner. Why don't we just celebrate then?"

"Sounds good."

"Good night, Noah."

"Night, gorgeous."

That's what I fell asleep to, and that's what I dreamed of all night: my fair-haired, rough-and-tumble, frog-catching, kiss-stealing, promise-making friend.

Because the one part of the story neither of us mentioned was how he'd given me a small golden ring he'd saved up for all summer. It had a red apple on it because it was my favorite food in the entire world at ten, and he wanted me to think of him whenever I thought of my favorite things.

And then, he'd asked me to marry him.

CHAPTER FIFTEEN

ALL SHIT HIT the fan at work, and lunch with my grampa and Babs couldn't come soon enough. The office was in an uproar, seeing as Shay wasn't the only one let go. The cuts made sense, though, if I were being pragmatic and looking at the different departments from a financial perspective. It seemed like the entire company was getting a shake-up, not just the editorial division.

On a positive note, I was welcomed into the office that morning by the most amazing bouquet of flowers I'd ever seen sitting on my desk. I could only assume they'd come from Pierce as a congratulations. *You were born to sit among the stars! Congratulations, beautiful.* That's all the note said. It was nestled in a lush bouquet of verdant green botanicals, stunning white roses, and a surprising splash of color from sunny, tangerine-soaked calla lilies and tulips.

Everyone was excited for my promotion, and I was feeling inspired and creative as I brainstormed about how to reimagine the new romance department. I wasn't sure Shay's position truly needed to be replaced, but I wouldn't know for sure before I met with the rest of my new team. Based on preliminary projections and sales data, though, it looked as if Shay's workload had been on a steady decline over the last few years, despite her boastful claims.

Before I could corner Pierce and thank him for the flowers, I realized the morning had flown by and I needed to scooch if I wanted to make it to lunch on time. Grampa and Babs were waiting for me at the small sandwich shop close to Uptown. They had my favorite tuna on toasted whole grain. That, and freshly squeezed cherry limeades. Grampa liked their vanilla milkshakes and French dip sandwiches on soft white hoagies. They were his favorite in all of Charlotte.

"Hey, Grampa," I said, sitting down at the cozy little booth near the window. Freshly cut flowers filled a small mason jar and made me think of my own gorgeous arrangement back at the office.

The look of confusion that flashed over his eyes gutted me. Time stopped, and I willed him to recognize me. "Grampa?"

When nothing came, I inhaled sharply, glancing at Babs as I held back the fresh tears that were threatening to come forward.

Babs shook her head imperceptibly, tears already clouding her eyes.

I glanced between them, my grandfather now focusing on his silverware. He looked up at Babs, then at me. "Oh, do you have a friend joining us for lunch today?" he asked her. He reached out his hand across the checkered tablecloth. "I'm Lynwood Sterling."

I nodded, wiping the tears now falling down my cheeks. I shook his hand. "It's nice to meet you, Mr. Sterling."

"Please, call me Lynwood. Sterling's just the fancy name on my business cards."

"Oh?" I asked. "And where do you work?"

"I own a small publishing company. You might have heard about it?"

"Tell me about it," I said.

So, he did. Over lunch he told me all about the publishing company he and his wife started in Charlotte—one he hoped would compete with the Big Six in New York City one day. I used my napkin to wipe the tears as he spoke. He hadn't talked about Gramma Gracie in a long time—the stunning Graceland Masters who was on her way to New York City to become a famous author before Grampa stepped in and swept her off her feet!

"You'd like Gracie," he said. "You favor her. Do you know my Gracie?"

I bit the corner of my lip, feeling it tremble as I clutched the napkin. "She sounds wonderful, Lynwood. I hope your dreams come true."

His blue eyes brightened. "Oh, they will. I have the Midas touch. It runs in the family."

I lost it, the shaky laugh spilling from my lips as I swallowed more tears. I glanced at Babs. "Will you be all right with him today? Will you call me if anything changes?"

She nodded. "He was fine this morning," she said quietly, turning from him so only I could hear. Grampa went back to eating his sandwich, as if it was his first time. My tuna sandwich sat cold and untouched on my plate.

"It's time, isn't it?"

"He still has good days, Brynn. But I think it's time to either get a second nurse or go ahead and pull the trigger and get him in the retirement center. You just need to let me know what you want to do."

I nodded, grateful for Grampa's longtime caregiver. She'd known my gramma, too, before Gracie died.

"It was nice to meet you, Lynwood," I said, standing.

"You as well, darling."

It was two o'clock when I left the restaurant. Instead of going back into the office, I texted Lindy and asked her to cover for me. I couldn't go back yet. I needed time to breathe. To pull my shit together. I drove to Freedom Park and walked along the pathway, past the old coal-burning steam engine that was a permanent display in the park. Young children raced in and out of the conductor's chamber along the wooden walkway that led to the cozy space. I remembered Grampa taking me there as a kid—telling me stories about the old locomotive, and how it was gifted to the city.

I walked across the small bridge and over to the lake, drawing in deep lungfuls of air. The weather was still beautiful in Charlotte, despite it being November. It was one of the things that drew me back here after college. That, and the desire to carry on my grandfather's legacy. His dream had come true years ago when Sterling and Masters went public. He eventually sold his baby when my gramma died and he retired. It was a peaceful takeover, and the new corporation still held on to my grampa's original ideals. Not many people at work knew of my connection to the original Sterling and Masters, and I wanted to keep it that way. I wanted every ounce of my success to be mine.

My heart constricted at the thought of not being able to tell my grampa the good news about my promotion. He would be so proud of me. I knew the odds were good that he would have at least one good day again—at least, I hoped he would. But his incoherence today had decimated me. Without thinking, I picked up my phone and dialed.

"Brynn? Is everything okay?"

The floodgates opened, and I started to cry, my hand covering my mouth as my body shook against the wooden bench I'd fallen onto.

"Brynn, talk to me," he said.

I inhaled, trying to catch my breath enough to choke the words out. "Sorry. I didn't know who else to call. I panicked."

"Brynnie," Noah said, "you can call me anytime. What's wrong?"

"It's my grampa."

"Oh no," he said. "Do I need to hop on a plane and get there earlier?"

My heart stopped. "You'd do that for me?"

"Of course, pigtails," he said, trying to lighten the mood. "Tell me what happened."

So, I did. He didn't once say he was busy or tell me I'd interrupted anything. It would've been around seven in the evening his time, I realized. But he listened as I told him all about my grampa's condition and how he didn't recognize me today. I talked until my steam ran out and my heart felt heard.

"I'm so sorry," he murmured.

He didn't tell me how to fix it. He didn't tell me I was wrong or overreacting. He'd listened. The steady and dependable Noah I remembered and once loved. Yes, I'd been ten when I gave him my heart. But maybe I'd never gotten that small sliver back. I didn't know. I just knew that talking to Noah again made sense. It felt good and steady—and right now, I needed that, when everything else in my world was suddenly changing so fast.

"I'm glad I'll get to see you next week," I said, laughing through my tears and snot. I pulled a tissue from my purse and blew my nose. "I promise I won't be a basket case by then."

"You can be anything you need to be," he said affectionately. "Hey, did you get my surprise today? If not, I have a little something that may cheer you up when you get back to the office."

"Did you—did you send those flowers?" I asked, shocked.

"I did. I just wanted to say congratulations. I can't wait to celebrate with you in person."

"Me too," I said. "Noah—"

"It's okay. We can talk about everything later."

"I need to tell you something, though."

"Okay," he said.

"I—I just met someone. It's still really new."

"Brynn, you don't owe me an explanation. Let's just see what happens when I get there."

I nodded, though he couldn't see me as we chatted today.

"I won't push you. But I will fight for you—if your heart's available. Is it?"

"I don't know," I said. "I don't know what this is with this other guy yet. And I don't know what this is with you. I mean, we won't even know if any of this chemistry feels real until we see each other again, right? And it's not like anything can work long-term with us. You're in London, for god's sake."

"Brynnie," he said patiently, "you think I'd let something as silly as a little ocean come between us if I got a second chance with you?"

And there went the other half of my heart to Noah.

CHAPTER SIXTEEN

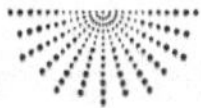

PIERCE WAS UNDERSTANDING when I texted him and told him I was taking the rest of the day off. I wasn't ready to see him yet when I was still so in my head and heart around Noah. How in the world had this happened in just a few short days? I knew what I had with Pierce was just physical. But he was in my space constantly—reminding me of the magnetic pull I had toward him.

I thought about the meeting that was on the books for Tuesday and how it would be just me, my childhood best friend who still held a flame for me, and my current fuck buddy—all nice and cozy in one small conference room.

I was hyperventilating and knew I needed to talk to Lindy.

She met me after work at the nail bar. She chose a light baby blue for her toenails, and I selected black. It fit my mood today. We each got a glass of white wine and sat back in our massage chairs while the technicians slathered our feet with orange-scented exfoliation lotion. It was the first time I relaxed all day.

"Thank you," I said to my best friend. "I needed this."

"I knew it was an SOS," she said, looking over at me. "You doing any better?"

I'd had the afternoon to calm down and think things through, so my heart *was* in a better place now than it was after my lunch with Grampa.

"I am," I said, smiling lightly. I gave her the CliffsNotes version of what went down and how I'd arrived at our favorite nail bar with a confused and divided heart.

"Wow, okay. So Noah, the dark horse, coming in on the last lap."

I laughed at her analogy. "Who would've thunk it, right? What am I going to do, Lindy? I mean, I need to talk to Pierce, but I want him to give Noah a chance, professionally speaking. I'm afraid if he knows about our past together, he'll go all alpha male on me and shut down any possible negotiations."

"Now, hold on, Brynn. Yes, he's all hot alpha male meets boardroom tycoon. But, and this is a big 'but,'" she said, grinning.

I rolled my eyes. "I bet it is."

"He's a professional. And based on my interactions and conversations with him so far, I've found him to be smart and successful, with a laser focus on what drives the market. He doesn't seem the type to let personal business get in the way of a golden opportunity."

"I hope not," I said. "Whether we get the deal or not, or whether we even want to offer her one, I just want Pierce to give Noah a fair shot."

"And what about you?" she asked. "Do you want to give Noah a fair shot?"

"I don't know, Lindy. This all snuck up on me. But the hard part—the part that's making me pause—is that it *still* feels like home with Noah, even after all this time. The second I saw his face last night, my heart felt at ease. He was the first person I called today when I was a wreck. What does that say?"

"That you need to call your *current* best friend next time?" she said, laughing.

I reached out my hand and squeezed hers. "I love you," I said. "Now, let's talk weddings and take my mind off all my boy drama!"

THAT NIGHT, PIERCE called me for the first time. My condo felt lonely, and all I could think about as I curled up on my sofa with a blanket was how I wished I really did have six cats, just like Anna Akana.

"Hey," I said quietly, trying to imagine what Pierce looked like right now and where he was.

"Hey yourself. Everything okay? I was worried about you today."

My heart.

"I'm better now," I said.

"Want to talk about it?"

I thought about it. Did I? Or did I want to continue keeping things easy and surface-level with Pierce? It would be so much easier that way.

But my heart. I had to start listening to it again.

"I would, actually."

"I was hoping you'd say that," he said, just as my doorbell rang.

"Hang on," I said. "Someone's at my door."

"I'll wait."

I fixed my robe and headed to the door, wondering who it was this late. When I peeked through the slats of my blinds, I saw a delivery guy standing there with a gigantic bouquet of fall flowers. My favorite. Huge palm-sized sunflowers, rich crimson roses, sunset chrysanthemums, dark green fall foliage, and a splash of winterberries for texture. Being a Scorpio, fall was my favorite time of year. And only Lindy knew that this was the type of arrangement I wanted to carry down the aisle one day.

She was the best.

I threw open the door, ready to sign for my flowers when the bouquet shifted, and Pierce stood there grinning at me. "Hey, beautiful."

My heart blew wide open into a million pieces, and I started crying.

"Shh," he said, reaching out to cup my face with one of his hands. I pressed my cheek into his palm and closed my eyes.

Why did he have to be so damn perfect?

"Can I come in?"

I nodded, laughing through my tears. It had been that kind of day.

"Sorry." I waved him into my townhouse and stepped aside so he could enter. "Those are gorgeous."

"So are you," he said. "Where can I set them?"

"How about in here?" I led him into my cozy living room and pointed to the pass-through bar off the kitchen. I'd be able to see them from any room in my downstairs space from there. He set them down, then walked over to me, his eyes raking in my white robe.

"Nice," he said, wrapping a hand around my waist and pulling me to him.

His other hand found refuge in my hair, and I sighed. I was wearing it down tonight, so it tumbled past my shoulders and halfway down my back. Just the feel of Pierce's fingers on my scalp triggered something so primal in me. He hadn't done anything overtly sexual—he was just holding me. But my entire body was on fire. *I* was on fire. And more than anything, I needed him.

I looked up into his midnight-blue eyes. "I need you to fuck me. My heart hurts tonight, and I want to talk to you about everything. But I need to forget first. I just need to feel," I said through my teary eyes.

His mouth crashed down around mine, and the world fell away. All of my problems. All of my fears. Every fractured piece of my heart flew back together, and I gave myself to Pierce. I led him up to my bedroom, which was the entire top floor. And for the rest of the evening, Pierce fucked away my pain. Then he kissed it and sewed it back together. It was nearly three in the morning the last time he made love to me. When we were done, and my body ached in the most delicious way possible, I rolled over and let him hold me until I'd nearly fallen asleep. I asked him sleepily if he'd stay the night. I *needed* him to.

That's how I ended up falling asleep with Pierce curled around me, the big spoon.

It shouldn't have surprised me, but we were a perfect fit.

CHAPTER SEVENTEEN

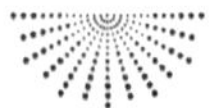

THE MORNING CAME too fast, but I kissed Pierce and sent him out the door. Luckily, I lived close to work and Uptown, so neither of us would be late. We'd be exhausted. But not late. Besides, I think the boss would give me a pass this one time.

When I stepped into my office, I was immediately reminded of Noah, his elegant bouquet of flowers still sitting front and center on my desk as if they'd just been delivered. I touched one of the petals, lost in thought.

"Should I be jealous?" Pierce asked from the doorway.

I turned, surprised to see him here already.

"They're from a friend," I said.

"The same friend who's on my calendar for Tuesday?" he asked point-blank.

I'd already told him that the deal was coming through an old friend—it was how we had the in, after all. "Yes," I answered simply, truthfully. I would never lie to Pierce or to Noah.

His eyebrows furrowed. "Do we need to talk about this, Brynn?"

I nodded. He came into the office and closed the door behind him. The blinds were still closed from yesterday, but I noticed he locked the door automatically.

"I didn't necessarily mean right now," I squeaked. "I still need to read the proposal for Tuesday, as well as Eve's first book in the series. Not to mention," I said, narrowing my eyes at him, "I now have an entire team I need to restructure and provide a little direction for."

"You'll get it all done," he said confidently. He sat down in one of my chairs and looked at me until I finally sighed and sat down next to him.

"Has anyone ever told you that you're stubborn?"

He laughed. "Every day of my life."

"Typical Leo," I said, but my heart had softened, and I was ready to open up to Pierce about everything.

"So, the gentleman we're meeting with on Tuesday is Noah Chance," I said.

"Yeah, I know, Brynn. I've done my homework. I know exactly who he is, who he works for, who his clients are, and what his track record is. I know his strengths and weaknesses on a professional level, and how he'll come into the negotiations on Tuesday. What I don't know is what he means to you."

Well, fuck. That didn't go as planned.

"He was my next-door neighbor growing up. We were best friends. Had innocent childhood crushes. That kind of thing. He moved to London with his family when he was twelve and I was ten. Like I said, we were young."

"And that's it? He just happens to turn up at our publishing house with a deal of a lifetime, demanding that you be in charge of the negotiations?"

"He never did that," I said. "He emailed me and let me know about the opportunity, asked if we could meet to discuss it. So, I set up the meeting with him."

"Yes, but when I contacted him directly this morning, he bristled hearing from anyone other than you. When I explained who I was and how you worked for *me*, he still didn't back down. He said the deal was non-negotiable unless the negotiations went through you. Mind explaining that?"

"I—can't," I said. "I mean, we're friendly still—"

"*How* friendly, Brynn?"

"I don't know, okay?" I practically shouted. I took a deep breath to calm the fuck down. I felt cornered, and I didn't like it one bit. "I haven't seen or heard from him in eighteen years, Pierce. But he was special to me. He *is* special to me. He'll always be a friend. That's all I know."

"But he wants you," he stated.

I shrugged. "I don't know that for sure."

"You're lying, Brynn."

"I don't lie, Pierce. And I'd be careful before you start accusing me of something I haven't even done yet." I stood up, getting more upset. "Besides, we don't have any strings attached, remember?"

He stood up next to me, his dark, midnight eyes bearing down into mine, gripping my soul and my heart in his hands. "What if I want the strings, beautiful?" he said, surprising me. He moved closer, running a hand down my hair and over my shoulder. "What if I want to complicate things and make them messy and call you mine?"

I shivered, my body betraying me. But it was more than that. After last night, I knew that if Pierce called me his, it would be body *and* soul. I knew he could meet me on any level I needed him. He'd held me, listened to me talk about my grampa and my fears, and then he'd kissed them all away. Buried himself deep inside of me until all I could see behind closed lids were the stars he was putting there.

"I'd like that," I said honestly. Pierce was only the second person I'd told about my ties to Sterling and Masters—Lindy being the other, of course. I think his respect for me tripled in size after that. I could feel the pride bubbling over as we talked about everything and how it was important to make my successes my own. Besides, it wasn't as if my grampa owned the company anymore. The key was, Pierce *got* me. He understood why I'd stuck with Sterling and Masters all this time. And why my heart was so damn invested.

"But I don't know if I can give them back just yet," I said, wishing the words were easier—or different. "Not until I know for sure that I can give them back a thousand percent, Pierce. I won't be a cheater or a liar. I've had one of those before. My heart doesn't work that way. And I'm starting to care about you. A lot, considering how little time I've actually known you."

"Yeah, but you know as well as I do that some things are just meant to be, Brynn. You felt it, too, when I took you in my arms that first time. Sometimes home is a person, not a destination. And your body is my home, Brynn. I can't explain it, but I *feel* it with everything I have. But it's not enough for me. I want your heart too."

He gathered me in his arms and soothed me, rubbing my back as we stood there, molded together. It was reckless to think about giving anyone my heart this fast. Especially someone I'd just met.

So why, then, did it feel like he already had a good chunk of it?

CHAPTER EIGHTEEN

THE WEEK FLEW by in a blur. Pierce took me out again on Friday night, and we met up with Lindy and Walter for drinks and dancing afterward. Walter and Pierce got along smashingly and had no problem finding common ground to talk about while Lindy and I gabbed all things wedding.

I was nervous about Tuesday, but I didn't let it stop me from exploring what Pierce and I were cautiously building. Brick by brick, we were building a foundation. I just hoped Hurricane Noah didn't come in and tear everything to the ground.

Noah and I talked a few times that weekend too. But I didn't meet him any further than my heart was able. For once, I was determined not to let my heart get swept away, but to be patient until I could see him again in person. Then, my heart would know.

Meanwhile, Pierce did everything he could to convince me of our connection, and it was working. I'd spent nearly the whole rest of the week in his hotel room—and in his bed. Okay, so maybe not *just* in his bed. I mean, we *had* to revisit the sauna. We broke in the bathtub too. And his hotel room desk. The small built-in bar. And the large sofa overlooking the city below. Pierce had rearranged the furniture and placed the gigantic black-tufted couch right in front of the large floor-to-ceiling windows. Then, one night, he turned off all the lights and closed the privacy blinds almost all the way, leaving a space big enough for us to see out of. Then, he'd turned me around and fucked me hard up against the glass window, the stars our only witnesses.

He was wooing me too. When I mentioned how I was considering getting a cat, he drove me to the shelter on Saturday to look at kittens. I let him drive my grampa's Rolls, and he looked awfully smooth behind the wheel. I didn't know if I would find a kitten I connected with, but it appeared I had a little love left in my heart to spare.

A tiny white and greige-colored runt caught my eyes—maybe because, like Pierce, her eyes were a striking shade of blue. The lady at the front said a litter was brought in by a woman who had found the kittens on a golf course. She wasn't certain, but based on her markings, and those of her brothers and sisters, she was most likely a mix between a Persian and a Ragdoll—quite rare to find at a shelter. So, even though it meant a lot of fur, I snatched her right up. She had me at hello when I nuzzled her close to my ear and asked her if she wanted a forever home. Her happy little motor purring in my ear was the only confirmation my heart needed.

If only men were so easy.

"I'll take her," I said and filled out the paperwork.

That night, Pierce slept at my house again so we could snuggle with Gracie. I knew right away when I first saw her what her name would be. I wasn't sure it was normal, but I gave her a full and proper name: Graceland Lucine

Hartley. It didn't take long for me to indoctrinate her as a full Southern girl and start calling her by her two first names—Gracie Lucine!

All weekend, we played house, and I was getting a little too comfortable with it. I was able to put Noah in my back pocket and focus on my connection with Pierce. I needed to figure out if there was more than just our physical chemistry. That, we had in the bag.

The problem was, it didn't take a rocket scientist to know that the answer was yes. If Noah wasn't a factor, I knew for certain I would've thrown my heart to the wind by now and jumped both feet first into the deep end with Pierce.

Well, not that I hadn't already.

I just had a hunky lifeguard waiting on shore for me if I needed saving. And that lifeguard was in town as of Monday night, making it hard for me to get my head in the game by the time Tuesday rolled around.

I was at the office bright and early that morning, getting everything ready. Pierce and I had spent all day Monday poring over the proposal, the number projections, and the manuscript, looking for any holes. We'd had Legal draft a contract with room for improvisation, just in case. It was a risky move, but I could tell Pierce was thinking with his career and not his dick.

That was, until Noah walked through the conference room door. The moment I laid eyes on him, I realized I'd been fooling myself all this time.

"Noah!" I said, standing. Pierce also stood, but I could tell by his posture that he was not amused. I walked over to my long-lost friend and gave him a quick hug. The only problem was, Noah didn't let go. He held on to me far too long for a professional gesture, and I suddenly wanted a hole to open up in the conference room floor and swallow me.

It wasn't that I didn't enjoy his arms around me, but the daggers I felt in my back from Pierce made me realize what a horrible decision this had been to put them both in the same room together. *Why* had I thought I could pull this off?

Because the truth was, if Pierce hadn't been there, I would've held on even longer.

Noah finally pulled back, holding my hands as he gave me a once-over. "You're a sight for sore eyes," he said.

Then he reached out a hand to Pierce—who stood there stony-eyed, taking in our little reunion.

"Noah Chance," he said. "Chance and Chambers Creative. You must be Mr. Abrams."

Sir.

I looked between the men in my life, my hormones on overdrive and warning bells firing in my head.

Pierce shook his hand briskly, then gestured for Noah to take a seat.

"Miss Hartley is our new romance editorial executive, so as such, I'm giving her full carte blanche over this deal," he said, surprising me. "She has the final decision on whether or not Sterling and Masters wants to acquire Miss Donohue's new series. It was nice to meet you, Mr. Chance."

With that, Pierce left the conference room, leaving Noah and me in stunned silence. He looked at me, then looked at the door, his jaw hardening.

"Why didn't you tell me, Brynn?"

"What do you mean?"

"You know damn well what I mean," he said. "Pierce? Really?"

"I did," I said quietly. "I told you I'd met someone else and it was a little complicated."

"Yeah, but you didn't tell me you were fucking your boss. That's a whole other level of complication. Especially when my client's future is on the line."

"Luckily for you, I know how to keep my personal and my business emotions separate. Do you?"

His jaw twitched, and I saw the successful literary agent behind his gorgeous hazel eyes for the first time. He was here to negotiate, not date.

We hammered out the deal over the next few hours, and I thought long-term with my business brain and not my heart—or my vagina. The truth of the matter was that Donohue was a huge gamble for Sterling and Masters. But at the end of the day, with great risk comes great reward. And I'd done my homework.

By one o'clock, we'd signed the paperwork and reached a deal. It just needed Pierce's final signature for the financial piece, so I told Noah I would have it signed and couriered over to his hotel later that evening.

"It was a pleasure doing business with you, pigtails," he said, relaxing for the first time since he'd walked in our doors.

I grinned and reached out to shake his hand and seal the deal, when he pulled me back into his arms. I glanced at the office door nervously. The negotiation room was the only office space on our floor without window walls. It was a war room, where utmost privacy was expected and required. Unfortunately, it also left me utterly defenseless in Noah's arms.

"Do you have any idea how sexy you are when you negotiate?" he said, hugging me fiercely. "I don't like the way he looked at you."

I glanced up at Noah. "What do you mean?"

"Pierce," he said protectively. "You sure he's got your back at the end of the day? Or will he stab you in it for the next big deal?"

"That's not fair. You don't know Pierce like I do."

"I thought it was still new with him. Has something changed?" he asked.

What could I say? Yes? No? Maybe?

"Let me guess—it's complicated."

I grinned sadly. "It is. But that doesn't mean I don't want to see you while you're here or that we can't spend time together. I've missed you."

"And your watchdog doesn't mind if I take you out on a date tomorrow night?" he growled.

"I make my own decisions, Noah. Pierce and I aren't exclusive yet."

"Yet." Noah gazed down at me. Those eyes. I'd spent so many hours as a kid looking into them. They were wiser now. A little harder, more mature. And somehow, both sexier and softer at the same time. They belonged to a man who knew how to treat a woman. Gone was the uncertain boy who had kissed me that first time.

"Still have your engagement ring?" he asked, smirking.

I swatted him. "You're awful, Noah Chance."

"But I think you still like it," he whispered. "Maybe just a little?"

His head dipped, and before I knew what was happening, my eyes were closing, and I gave my lips over to my childhood crush again, for the first time after eighteen years. He held my head possessively, as if he were afraid to let me go. His tongue swept my lips gently, testing the waters and giving me time to relearn his terrain.

Then he cupped my head tighter and pressed his tongue forward, parting my lips to find my own. The spark was instant and unlike anything we'd felt in that tentative kiss back on Operation Goodbye day. Our tongues explored cautiously at first, finding our pace. I wrapped my arms around his broad back, swooning over the changes in his body. He'd had eighteen years to fill out—and had he ever.

As he tasted me, teased me, I realized how different his kiss was from Pierce's—they were like night and day. Unfortunately, you need both to make the world go round, and how I would ever choose was beyond me. Where Pierce's was forged in fire, Noah's was grounded in sensuality. My Leo and my Taurus.

One of fire, one of earth.

Both with the potential to break my heart.

CHAPTER NINETEEN

PIERCE BARELY LOOKED up when I knocked on his office door.

"Have a minute?" I asked.

He finally put his pen down and sighed, looking up at me. He looked stressed for the first time since I'd met him. He was always nothing less than powerful, confident, and in control. Now, he looked vulnerable, and my heart couldn't handle the responsibility.

"Did we get the deal?"

I grinned and waved the signed contract in the air.

"I knew you would be a fierce negotiator," he said, grinning back for the first time. "Come here."

His command was a question—just like the day he'd asked me to kneel for him on his office floor. I'd submitted then. Would I do it again?

In that moment, with our eyes transfixed on one another, I knew.

I would always go to Pierce Abrams.

I knew it in my bones as I crossed the room to his desk. Noah had a part of my heart, but I was afraid Pierce may've captured my entire soul.

I set the contract down in front of him. When he patted his knee, I about lost it. I curled up on his lap, wrapping my arms around his neck. His shoulder was the perfect place for my head, so I let myself sink into his comfort.

"Mine," he said, low and possessive.

He found my mouth, ravaging it, erasing any trace of Noah from my lips. I whimpered as he shifted me and lifted my skirt so I could straddle his lap. When he looked down, he noticed I was completely bare, having not replaced the underwear he'd confiscated.

"Christ, Brynn. You fucking negotiated a six-figure deal with no underwear on?"

I nodded my head, nipping at his lower lip.

"You know you're perfect, right?" he growled, freeing himself from his pants. He reached around me and grabbed a condom from his top desk drawer. Guess he knew he would be getting lucky more in the office.

He rolled the condom down with one hand, then held his cock, stroking it along the front of my pussy to wet the tip. "I can't wait, Brynn."

"Then don't," I said breathlessly, sinking my thighs over his cock and lowering myself to encase him. I stretched to hold him, to take him all the way in. His arms wrapped around me, holding the back of my head possessively as he helped lower me up and down over his straining cock.

It was as if we hadn't fucked in a week and were starved for one another. We both came fast and hard, my body arching away from Pierce's in total surrender. It was quick and dirty, and right in all the best ways.

Except for one.

I'd forgotten to lock his office door. And Noah chose that moment to knock and enter—before Pierce had a chance to answer.

Even though Pierce was fully clothed as far as Noah could tell, my ass was on full display, and there was no desk big enough to cover what we'd been up to.

I looked over my shoulder at my nighttime, my shadow. And knew in the worst way possible, I'd just broken his heart.

"Noah," I said. But my words were empty at this point. Meaningless.

"Congratulations, Brynn. Guess things don't have to be so complicated anymore."

With that, Noah shut the door on any possible different outcome as he left.

"Fuck!" I said, burying my head in Pierce's shoulder.

"Go after him."

I sat up, stunned. "What? No. It's not like that."

"But you'll always wonder, Brynn. And I won't ever be someone's second choice."

I swallowed, looking down at the man who had decimated my life and turned it upside down in such a short amount of time.

"Don't get me wrong. I want you more than I can even comprehend is possible. It's not logical. It doesn't make sense that my entire being can want you so badly, so entirely. I won't settle till I have you all to myself. For that to happen, you need to either explore what's there so you flush him from your system or just talk to the poor guy to say goodbye for good. Either way, you'll know what to do when you see him."

"How did I get so lucky?" I whispered.

"Must be fate," he said huskily.

I looked down at him and smiled. "Why, Mr. Abrams, are you telling me you believe in soul mates and stuff like that?"

His eyes drank me in, and he pressed my lower lip with his finger as if marking it one last time.

"I do now."

CHAPTER TWENTY

NOAH WOULDN'T ANSWER his phone or his texts. I couldn't blame him. He must've been so hurt and confused. I'd let myself get swept up in the gravitational pull that was Pierce, and I never stopped to make sure the door was locked. It was a rookie mistake, and unfortunately, one that cost me one of the dearest people in my life.

Because even if Noah didn't end up being *the one,* he was my *first one.* The boy I'd promised to marry if I was single by the time I was thirty. The only problem was, for the first time in my life, that no longer seemed like an issue. Whether I was or not, I was starting to like the life I was building here in Charlotte. And surprisingly, my "complication" was turning into something that made a lot more sense to me.

But I knew Pierce was right. I either had to exorcise Noah from my system and break his heart, or I had to be crystal clear on what my heart wanted from both him and my boss. I wouldn't string either of them along.

Noah never picked up, but around two thirty in the morning, he finally texted me—stone-cold drunk off his ass. And my heart ached knowing I was the sole reason for it.

NOAH: Brynnie . . . you there?
BRYNN: I'm here.
NOAH: Why? Why couldn't it be me?
BRYNN: Where are you?
NOAH: At my house. I mean, the hotel.
BRYNN: Are you okay?
NOAH: Would you be?
BRYNN: No.
BRYNN: I'm so sorry, Noah.
NOAH: You broke me, pigtails.

I choked out a cry, hot tears flooding down my face.

NOAH: You still there?
BRYNN: I'm here.
NOAH: I might be a little drunk.
BRYNN: How much did you drink?
NOAH: I don't know. I lost count. The bartender was counting, though.
BRYNN: And he cut you off?
NOAH: Yeah. Asshole.
BRYNN: But you're safe at the hotel now?
NOAH: Yeah. I'm fine. I'll be fine.
NOAH: Will you still go out with me tomorrow?
NOAH: I need to see you before I leave.
BRYNN: I'll be there for you, Noah.
NOAH: Thank you, pigtails. I knew you would be.

BRYNN: See you tomorrow at 6?
NOAH: That's good. You remember Loula Belle's house?
BRYNN: How could I forget? It was my favorite one ever.
NOAH: I'm gonna fall asleep now.
BRYNN: I think that's a good idea, Noah.
NOAH: I love you, Brynnie.
BRYNN: Get some sleep.

The flashing dots came up more than one time, letting me know he was typing a response and then deleting it more than once. They finally went away, and I figured he probably passed out. Either he was going to wake up in the morning and regret asking to still see me, or I was going to have the hardest conversation of my life.

Either way, I needed the gods to be with me.

I snuggled up with Gracie Lucine and cried myself to sleep, her soft, constant purring the one thing comforting my guilt-ridden heart.

PIERCE TOOK WEDNESDAY off, at least according to his PA, Alastor. I spent the day meeting with my team and brainstorming our new organization, the breakdown of roles, and what our first-quarter projections would be. For the rest of this year, we'd be finishing any open projects and closing out any contracts that were no longer aligned with our new direction. Things, at least on a work front, were looking up by the time I left the office.

I went home to change my clothes and get into something more comfortable. I didn't know where we were going, but I was pretty sure it would be somewhere laid back and low key.

I pulled up in front of Loula Belle's home, and my heart skipped a beat. The Historic Dilworth bungalow hadn't changed much since I'd last been there, but it had gotten a makeover. The java brown house sat close to the road like the other properties nearby, its classic cedar and stone exterior blending in nicely with the other renovations that had been done. A wildflower garden burst with color in front of the large signature open-air porch. The floor was painted red, and a fan was gently blowing the still night air around the space. Rocking chairs flanked the front door, and I had sudden and swift flashbacks of riding bikes back from the store with Noah, abandoning them on the front lawn to run in for a bottle of Cheerwine soda.

There were three things that were always certain at Loula Belle's house: Southern hospitality, Cheerwine, and a warm hug.

I was about to knock on the front door when I noticed Noah standing there, leaning against the door frame, and looking at me with all the longing of what might have been in his eyes. He pursed his lips sadly and held up a bottle of Cheerwine for me.

"Hey, Noah," I said, as he stepped onto the front porch, letting the screen door slam shut behind him.

"Hey yourself," he said, handing me the bottle. I missed the smile that met his eyes just yesterday. It was as if he knew he'd lost and the last quarter of the game was just too hard to fumble his way through.

"Can I get a hug?" I asked.

I was afraid he'd say no. I breathed a sigh of relief when he finally set his Cheerwine onto the front railing and came to me—a small sign that our friendship wasn't completely lost. I set my drink down, too, and glanced up at him shyly.

He wrapped his arms around me then, holding on tight as if he never wanted to let me go. I felt the hard planes of his chest as he crushed me against his body, drinking me in. He kissed the top of my head, then stepped back. It was over before I'd even had a chance to properly hug him back.

"Here," he said, pointing to the rockers. "Let's sit."

We both sat down, Noah looking out at the quiet neighborhood street. A lady jogged by with a double stroller and waved at us. We waved back.

"Can I start?" I asked. I didn't know how any of this was supposed to go, but I knew I owed Noah better.

"Sure," he said, rubbing his hands on his jeans.

I moved my rocker in front of his. "Noah, can you look at me at least?"

He steeled his jaw, still looking out at the street. Then he finally dragged his eyes to mine, and I noticed they were fresh with tears. He'd been crying.

"Fuck," I said, pulling in a deep, ragged breath.

"It's fine, Brynn. Really."

"No, it's not. I owe you the biggest apology ever."

"You don't," he said sadly. "That's the thing. I had a lot of time yesterday, last night, and today to think about things. You didn't seek me out. I found *you*. I'm the one who came back for *you*."

"That doesn't change the fact that I was excited about hearing from you," I said.

"No, but you also don't owe me anything, just because we were friends once. No matter how much I've romanticized you over the years, we're not the same people anymore. We weren't dating. Hell, I'd only just seen you again for the first time after eighteen years."

"Yeah, but I shouldn't have let you kiss me when my feelings were so torn."

"Maybe not, but I don't regret that kiss. It reminded me of what's been missing from my life and how badly I want it again."

"Just not with me?" I said, suddenly realizing we'd landed on the same page.

"Someone as amazing as you, yes." He smiled for the first time. "But you know what I noticed yesterday?"

"What?"

"Your feelings were never really torn. I knew that the second I walked into that conference room and was slammed with the intensity of your connection with Pierce. It was a dick thing to do—to kiss you. To take what I knew wasn't mine. But I had to know, Brynn." He ran his hand through his blond hair. "I owe you an apology for that."

"Noah," I said, reaching out.

"It's okay. Things are a lot clearer to me now. I'll be fine. I'm glad I got to see you while I was in town, and before I close the last chapter on my life here in the States for good."

I looked at the "For Sale" sign in the front yard, and my heart dipped as I saw the fresh, new "SOLD" label slapped over the realtor's name.

"Wow," I said, "that was fast."

"Let's just say I priced it to sell. I needed to tie these loose ends, and I found someone who I know will love this house, this property, as much as I did growing up. That's all I could ever ask for," he said, looking through the screened door and into the house.

That's when I saw him.

My Pierce was standing in Loula Belle's kitchen with a Cheerwine in his hand.

I looked back at Noah, my eyes widening.

"Let him take care of you, Brynn. Apart, you're both powerhouses. Together, you'll be unstoppable. He loves you, you know."

I shook my head. He couldn't possibly. We hadn't known each other long enough. But we had room now, with Noah stepping back, to explore the possibilities and figure it out.

"Go on in. This was always the date you were meant to have here."

Tears brimmed in my eyes as I hugged Noah one last time, my eyes fixed and glued to Pierce's the entire time.

Noah glanced back into the house one last time before leaving. "London's only a seven-hour plane ride away, Abrams. You hurt her, I'll make a special return flight just for you."

Pierce actually nodded.

"Take care of my girl," Noah said, rubbing my arm one last time.

"You mean *my* girl," Pierce warned low.

"She was always yours," Noah said as he walked off the front porch.

I stood there in disbelief, not understanding what was really happening, but knowing for sure that my future was on the other side of the familiar screen door.

I held Pierce's steady blue gaze, opened the door, and stepped toward my future.

CHAPTER TWENTY-ONE

PIERCE DIDN'T MAKE me wait. He closed the gap between us and picked me up into his strong arms, twirling me around in the cozy living room I remembered. Except Loula Belle's fancy gold couch was no longer there, and the fireplace had been painted white—a natural, raw mantel warming the space. The bay window still held a reading nook, only it had been updated and was now larger and much more magical looking. A booklover's dream, I thought, soaking in the matching white built-ins flanking the fireplace.

I slid down Pierce's body, my arms wrapping around his head. "Mind explaining to me what you're doing here? In my childhood best friend's late grandmother's home?"

He laughed. "Well, when you put it that way."

I stood back, putting my hands on my hips. "Well?"

"How about this? I'll explain everything . . . if you come out in the backyard with me."

I narrowed my eyes at him. "What's the catch?"

"It's a date. I want to explain everything, but I want to woo you, too. Do you trust me?"

I rolled my eyes. "I think we've established that I do."

"Good," he said, grinning. "Then you won't mind putting this back on." He pulled the same silk tie out of his jeans' pocket that he'd put over my eyes the first weekend we'd met.

I swallowed nervously, glancing around. "Boy, I don't know what game you're playing, but I am *not* doing that here."

Pierce burst out laughing. "I said *trust* me, not *fuck* me. Though," he said, shrugging, "I wouldn't say no."

"The last time you said 'trust me' and covered my eyes, I got it up the ass," I reminded him.

"Oh my god," he said, laughing. "I will never grow tired of you."

My insides melted just a tad. "Good," I said and stepped forward. "Then tie me up, *sir*."

"Jesus, Brynn. You can't say stuff like that when I'm trying to be romantic."

I paused and looked into his eyes. They were filled with an emotion I'd not seen on Pierce before, and my heart started moshing in my chest. I closed my eyes, tilting my head back for him.

I felt his warm, steady fingers secure the tie around my eyes. Then his hand rested firmly on my lower back. He was leading me once again, and this time, I was completely at his mercy. He guided me through the house and onto the back porch. I could smell fresh honeysuckle and wisteria in the crisp evening air. It was dark now, and the crickets were sending their mating calls across the yard. It felt like home.

He stood behind me, wrapping his arms around my waist and leaning in close to my ear. He moved my hair from over my shoulder, his fingers brushing my bare throat. "I have a little surprise for you."

I wet my lips, eager to see what it was.

He ran his hand up my spine and to my hair, and I dropped my head back against his palm. My nipples were standing at attention, but I willed my damn hormones to take a back seat for once. He was trying to be romantic. I could let the poor man romance me for a hot minute, couldn't I?

"You're making it so hard for me, Brynn," he warned.

"Stop touching me, then," I whispered back.

"Never."

He bit my neck gently, a love nibble with a hot little sting that went straight south, then he soothed the skin with his warm tongue. I moaned, rolling my head back.

"Seriously, Pierce," I said. "Unless you intend to fuck me right here and right now, please stop touching me this way."

He chuckled and pressed himself against my ass. "Oh, I intend to have you tonight. But first, the romance," he said, undoing my blindfold.

I blinked, not understanding what I was seeing.

Fairy lights hung from the low branches of the ancient trees, decorating the entire backyard. In the center of the yard, a large movie screen hung from thick ropes secured over a low, sturdy branch—one I used to climb on with Noah.

Beige futon cushions that looked like sitting beds were parked in front of the screen, and a picture of me and Pierce from our mural tour filled the large white canvas. Spiked metal drink holders were drilled into the ground next to the futons, and little bottles of wine were nestled inside. I clapped my hands, noticing the popcorn tubs between the seats.

Rattan lanterns hung from the branches over the mattress seats, and colorful pillows of all shapes and sizes littered the yard.

I spun on my heel to look up at him. "Pierce, what in the world is all of this? You did this for me? And Noah let you? Why?"

It was the most magical thing a man had ever done for me.

Pierce nodded, holding my hand and leading me to the futons. "Come here," he said and patted his lap again. The man really needed to stop doing that.

I curled up in his lap, though, glad now that I'd worn my jeans, a Brooks Brothers polka dot dress shirt, and my favorite Vineyard Vines black cashmere sweater with large white stars on the front. I was cozy in Pierce's arms. He'd had me all kinds of twisted up after that first night. But now, I was content for the first time since we'd met.

Because I knew that no matter what came next, he was *mine.*

"I talked a long time to Noah today," he said, surprising me. "He called me and asked for a meeting, but not at the office."

"So that's why you weren't there today," I said.

"Yeah," he said, tucking my hair over my shoulder. "I didn't want to hear anything he had to say to me when it came to you. I knew you'd work through whatever you needed to with him. I was terrified you wouldn't choose me, but I trusted you."

"Thank you," I said.

"Noah's a nice guy," he said, surprising me again. "And he loves you, Brynn, whether it's as old friends or new friends. It doesn't matter. He's like family. You grew up with him—I get that now. He explained that you don't have a lot of family left, just your grampa. So, I get it now. He's a part of what made you who you are."

I nodded. "What did he want to talk to you about?"

"You. This house. Everything. He could see how I looked at you yesterday. He could see it in my eyes when I showed up here today to fight for you."

I grinned. "You were gonna fight for me?"

"Well, I wasn't gonna deck the guy or anything," he said, nuzzling my throat and eliciting a giggle from me. "Stop it, woman."

"Sorry," I said. "But all this alpha caveman testosterone seems to have a very strong effect on my libido."

Pierce barked in laughter. "Good, you better get used to it."

"And why exactly is that?"

"Because I plan to stay," he murmured.

"What?" I pulled back to look at him. "As in Charlotte? For good?"

"Why is that so hard to believe?"

"Because you're Mr. New York," I reminded him. "And because you said your role wasn't permanent."

"No, I said me filling in for Carlisa wasn't permanent. But Sterling and Masters *is*."

"Okay," I said, confused. "What am I missing, Pierce?"

"I didn't step into Carlisa's role so I could be an editorial executive," he said. "It was a way for me to get up close and personal with not only that team but all the different divisions there. Remember when I told you I'd met with Carlisa before she went on maternity leave? And how I was at Havana's with my lawyers and some investors?"

"Yeah?"

"It's because I'm buying out Sterling and Masters, Brynn. We're doing a takeover."

"Excuse me?"

"Meet your new CEO."

I sat back, taking him in. I nodded slowly, though my entire world just flipped upside down again because of Pierce. He had a way of doing that.

I socked him in the chest.

"Ouch!" he said. "What'd you do that for?"

"You *knew* you were going to be the CEO? And you let me *fuck* you in the office?"

"I didn't let you do anything, baby girl," he said huskily. "You fucked me too."

"You're right," I admitted, taking a deep breath. "But it's one thing to fuck my boss—and another altogether to be banging the CEO."

Pierce laughed. "Oh, is that what this is?" he asked, sweeping his hand around the backyard. "You think I'm settling for a little sex?"

"A little sex?" I asked, quirking a brow. "You mean the best sex you've ever had?"

"That too," he said, covering my mouth with his, his hands fisting my hair and consuming me once again. I was lost in his mouth, his tongue, his heart. He was handing it all to me on a silver platter. He wanted the strings, that much was abundantly clear.

"So, Mr. CEO. What are we doing, then? Watching a movie in Noah's backyard? This is how you woo me?"

"No, Brynn," he said, "this is how I woo you."

He pressed play, and the screen came to life. There were pictures of my childhood home and Pierce's. Pictures of us both growing up. The place where we first met. The night of the Heart Gala. Me in my angel wings. Pierce as Zorro.

I laughed. "How did you get these?"

"I'm a man with a great number of tricks up my sleeves, angel."

"Yes, you are," I said breathily.

He kissed me again, his hands roaming my body, distracting me.

Then I saw a picture on the screen that caught my eye and made me do a double take. It was my grampa. There was a picture of him and my gramma at Sterling and Masters back in the day. And one of him now with Babs. The picture of me sleeping came next, the one that he sent to Lindy so she would know I was safe.

Then there was a photo of Noah and Pierce shaking hands in front of the house—in the same clothes they were both in today. And one of me and Gracie Lucine that he'd taken this past weekend after I got her. But the best one was last. It was a photoshopped picture of Pierce and me, Gracie Lucine at our feet. Only, we were standing on Loula Belle's front porch, a big heart drawn around us.

I turned to gape at Pierce. What was he saying? It was too soon. He couldn't mean *that.*

"Brynn, take a deep breath. I'm not proposing."

I exhaled.

He laughed harder. "Good thing I don't actually have a ring on me."

"So, what *are* you saying, Pierce?"

"First of all, I want you to know that I know how much you love your grampa. As the new CEO, I think it's important for me to make sure you know that we may be making some changes, but we aren't losing the integrity of the company that Lynwood Sterling and Graceland Masters built.

"Secondly, Noah told me this was your favorite house in Charlotte—that it felt like a home away from home when you were little. He explained the situation, and how he needed to sell it fast. Well, I just so happen to need a new home so I can stay here in Charlotte. So, I made a cash offer on it today. We can figure things out later, but I want to be clear. I bought this house for you. I *want* you to live here with me someday—whenever you're ready. I know it's all still so new, but something tells me that we have something pretty magical happening between us. I *know* you feel it too."

I nodded, cupping his face in my hands.

"I was planning on coming to Charlotte, doing a takeover without getting my hands too dirty, and then heading back to New York. Then I saw you—and in that moment, it felt like I'd found a piece I didn't know was missing in my life. I'd never felt the need to *have* someone like that. All of them. And yeah, it's the best sex of my life. But it's more than that. You're the best *you* of my life. Somehow, beyond explanation, you charmed me off my feet, beautiful.

"I can't explain it, but I madly, completely, passionately, deeply love you, Brynn Graceland Hartley. And I want all the strings attached," he said, pulling something from his pocket.

He held two red strings, one with a small silver heart charm with a diamond twinkling from the center. "Have you ever heard of the red string?" he asked. When I shook my head, he continued.

"The red string represents the end of a spiritual journey. Like a decision, or an internal battle overcome. It also signifies living in the present moment, in a state of love. They're said to be worn by *destined* lovers—regardless of time, place, or circumstance. Our love story, Brynn, is just beginning. I'm not asking you for forever *yet,* but I know we'll have it. I feel it in my bones, and I know you do too."

Gentle tears fell from the corners of my eyes as I nodded. I'd never felt more certain of anything in my life. It defied logic, but there was a familiarity and longing with Pierce that I couldn't ignore.

"Will you have me, Brynn? With all the strings attached? Just you and me? I need to know you're willing to give this thing a real go."

I dropped my mouth to his and devoured him this time. I took everything I'd ever wanted and didn't know was in my reach. I licked his lips, kissed his neck, buried my face in his hair.

"I love you, too, Pierce Gregory Abrams," I said. "That red thread? It's the magnet I feel drawing me to you every time I'm near you, and even when I'm not. I want the strings too," I whispered, my voice thick with emotion.

He tied the red string around my wrist, and I tied his for him.

"They say you can never take this off, Brynn," he said. "It can wear off, and that's good luck. But your destined lover must always tie the new one back on your wrist."

I glanced down at my pretty bracelet and gasped. "Please tell me that's not a real diamond, then."

Pierce handed me a small wooden box and said, "Open it."

Inside, the box was full of red string bracelets, some with diamonds, some without. Enough to last a lifetime. Taped to the lid of the box was a key to the house.

"I'm not going anywhere, Brynn. And don't worry about the diamonds. I'm a CEO, remember?"

"You're not just *a* CEO," I told him. "You're *my* CEO."

He grinned, yanking me firmly onto his lap.

"Your CEO is ready to celebrate," Pierce growled.

Let's just say, I could already tell.

The screen went black and was full of nothing but golden stars dancing across the projector, darkening the backyard. He pressed himself up against me—and I was beyond ready for my guy.

"Take me home," I whispered in his ear, eager to have him slide inside me.

"We *are* home," he whispered back.

I looked over his shoulder and saw six little words dancing across the screen:

It was written in the stars.

THE END

WRITTEN IN THE STARS SERIES

Reluctant in Love by Rebecca Gallo
(Written in the Stars Book 1) https://amzn.to/2VBXggo

Bittersweet Love by Q.B. Tyler
(Written in the Stars Book 2) https://amzn.to/2y1ny2r

Daring to Love by Karen Ferry
(Written in the Stars Book 3) https://amzn.to/2VYhNuy

Price of Love by Erica Marselas
(Written in the Stars Book 4) https://amzn.to/2zxVpAD

Intrigued by Love by Sienna Snow
(Written in the Stars Book 5) https://amzn.to/2xYgl3a

Drowning in Love by Kelsie Rae
(Written in the Stars Book 6) https://amzn.to/2Y9ilAm

Fearless to Love by Harlow Lane
(Written in the Stars Book 7) https://amzn.to/3cS0IJI

Jaded by Love by AJ Alexander
(Written in the Stars Book 8) https://amzn.to/2yMb8vk

Balanced in Love by Jennifer Woodhull
(Written in the Stars Book 9) https://amzn.to/2VokGp8

Consumed by Love by C.M. Albert
(Written in the Stars Book 10) https://amzn.to/2S8DR10

Wandering in Love by Andi Jaxon
(Written in the Stars Book 11) https://amzn.to/2SbvCEV

Crashing into Love by Hollis Wynn
(Written in the Stars Book 12) https://amzn.to/2xOYVpT

OTHER BOOKS BY C.M. ALBERT

Arden's Glen Romances—
a stand-alone small-town romance series
Faith in Love
Proof of Love
Visions of Love

Stand-alone Books
Last Night in Laguna
The White Room

The Love in LA Quartet
Book 1 – The Stars in Her Eyes

ACKNOWLEDGMENTS

They're probably getting sick of me by now, but I literally could not function without Marisa Wesley from Cover Me Darling and Erin Servais of Dot and Dash, LLC. Thank you for your consistent help over the years to help make what I do easier, prettier, and the best it can possibly be for my readers. A special thank you to Crystal Shelley of Dot and Dash, LLC. This was our first time working together, and I'm hoping it won't be our last. They say you can't teach an old dog new tricks, but this retired editor appreciated your fresh perspective and my book is stronger because of it. Extra special thanks as well to Stephanie Anderson of Alt 19 Creative for helping me with formatting at the eleventh hour. I'm so happy to have met you and look forward to working together again soon!

I also want to thank Christopher John of CJC Photography. He's one of my favorites ever, and somehow this is my first cover working with him. It definitely won't be the last. I'd also like to thank cover models B.T. Urruela and Rachael Baltes. Likewise, this was my first cover with them, but as soon as I saw this smoking hot image, I knew I had to have it for *Consumed by Love.* The feelings this image stirred are actually what made me decide to have Brynn end up with Pierce instead of Noah. True story. It takes a team, and I had the best one for this cover!

An additional thank you goes to Kate Farlow of Y'all! That Graphic. This was my first time working with her, and I was blown away by all the sexiness she created for the entire Written in the Stars series. You're the brightest star in the sky!

I also want to thank the eleven extraordinary women and authors in the Written in the Stars series. This started as a dream of mine back in late summer, early fall of 2019. When I first started approaching my friends with this "crazy idea I have" for a branded horoscope series, you know what they all said? "I'm on board! Count me in!" Slowly, our collective of writers grew until we filled each zodiac sign, and from there, the magic was born. It may not have always been the smoothest ride to wrangle a group of insanely talented and wildly creative women, but we all learned a lot about our strengths and weaknesses along the way. The end result was a lot of teamwork, a lot of give and take, and an amazing collection of novellas I am so proud of and amazed by. You ladies forever have my gratitude and a special place in my heart: Rebecca Gallo (Aquarius), Q.B. Tyler (Pisces), Karen Ferry (Aries), Erica Marselas (Taurus), Sienna Snow (Gemini), Kelsie Rae (Cancer), Harlow Layne (Leo), A.J. Alexander (Virgo), Jennifer Woodhull (Libra), Andi Jaxon (Sagittarius), and Hollis Wynn (Capricorn). I am floored by the creativity and heart you each poured into your stories, and I am so grateful for each of you.

I also want to thank every book blogger, bookstagrammer, friend, reader, fellow author, designer, and PR company who has helped spread the word about my books and this entire new series. I could not do what I do without each of you. You literally are my glue, my fuel, and my inspiration. I love you madly.

A special shout-out to Bare Naked Words for managing our book tour promotions and blogger ARCs for the Written in the Stars series, and A.J. Alexander for managing our reader group ARC team.

Thank you, too, for the friends I've made this year in the most unexpected ways. Each of you has a piece of my heart. To my tight inner circle—Deena, Erin, Heather, Jacque, Jen, and Sheila—I love you each as soul mates of my heart. Thank you for being there for me this year in all the hard times and all the good times and all the boring times in between that make life so beautiful and fun and messy and perfectly imperfect.

I also want to thank my children for being the most amazingly supportive, funny, sweet, driven, inspiring, creative, and curious little souls. If Daddy was written in the stars for me, then I believe so were you. My world would not be complete without you. You make every day worthwhile. Thank you for being patient with me over summer break, and during a pandemic no less, when I told you I had to write not only one book but two. Thank you for putting up with me when I growled about leaving me alone because I was writing. I love you to Mars and back, Lil' G; and E, I love you to Pirate Island and back.

Derek . . . we've come a long way, baby. "If kisses were stars, I'd give you the sky." The universe may be limitless, but it still can't eclipse my love for you. It's u+me forever. Ours is definitely the greatest love story ever *written in the stars.*

ABOUT THE AUTHOR

USA Today bestselling author C.M. Albert writes heartwarming romances that are "sexy and flirty, sweet and dirty!" Her writing infuses a healthy blend of humor, high-heat romance, and—most of all—hope. When not writing or kid-wrangling, she's either meditating, kayaking, reading, hugging a tree, or asleep. But first, coffee. #TonyStarkForever

Join C.M. Albert online at:

WEBSITE: www.colleenalbert.com

WRITTEN IN THE STARS READER GROUP: https://www.facebook.com/groups/writteninthestarsbooks

FACEBOOK: https://www.facebook.com/cmalbertwrites

READER GROUP: https://www.facebook.com/groups/ColleensAngels

INSTAGRAM: https://www.instagram.com/cmalbertwrites

TWITTER: https://twitter.com/colleenmalbert

GOODREADS: https://www.goodreads.com/cmalbert

BOOKBUB: https://www.bookbub.com/profile/c-m-albert

PINTEREST: https://www.pinterest.com/cmalbertwrites

NEWSLETTER: https://www.subscribepage.com/w5x4p1

www.ingramcontent.com/pod-product-compliance
Lightning Source LLC
Chambersburg PA
CBHW030743110726
47900CB00008B/2435
9781733703352